SWEET INDULGENCE

CHARLESTON HARBOR NOVELS

DEBBIE WHITE

Editing provided by Daniela Prima of Prima Editing & Proofreading Services

Cover Design by Larry White

PROLOGUE

$\mathcal{T}$hey were known as the tough as nails McPherson sisters. They got it honestly too, with a grandmother who didn't pull any punches and an auntie who was as cool as a cucumber on the exterior but strong as a lioness when it came to protecting her cubs, Annie and Mary. They only wanted the best for the girls and that included the men in their lives.

Carefree and traipsing around Europe thanks to a very generous graduation gift, Mary wasn't about to let her loving but eccentric grandmother and auntie find her next beau.

Strong and determined, Annie had her hands full running a new cupcake bakery in town. Business was booming, and men, well, they were the last thing on her mind—especially the ones her grandmother and auntie tried to set her up with. But then, in walks Jack and everything Annie ever thought she knew about men went straight out the Sweet Indulgence door.

Can Annie focus on developing a relationship with Jack? Will her grandmother and auntie even let her? She may be twenty-six years old but they still treated her like she was sixteen. Perhaps Mary could take one for the team while Annie learned the lesson true love can't be decided for you. You, and you alone are in control of your happily ever after.

CHAPTER 1

*A*nnie watched as Morgan exited the bakery. As she turned to walk behind the counter, she heard the door open. Expecting it to be Morgan, Annie whirled around, getting ready to tease her about forgetting something, and instead locked eyes with a tall, dark, and handsome man.

"Good day," he said.

Annie's sparkling green eyes widened. She didn't recognize him, but then again, Sweet Indulgence had only been in business for three months. Her eyes traveled down his body and back up again. *Nothing like a smartly dressed man in a dark suit.* "How can I help you?"

The handsome man reared his head back and laughed. Annie let out a small giggle. "What's so funny?" Her hand frantically flew up to her face as she made a wiping motion. She'd been known to fling flour around and get it on anything and everyone.

"How can I help you?" The man cocked his head to one side and a broad smile swept across his mouth as he eyed the confectioner's paradise before him.

"Oh, yeah. I guess you want some cupcakes." Annie lowered her gaze.

"Yes, I do. In fact, two dozen, please."

Annie raised her eyes to meet his. "Do you want a variety?" She scanned the recently baked cupcakes.

"Sure, sounds good, mix them up." He stepped back from the counter and looked around. His eyes landed on Buffy. "What a cute little dog. Is she your guard dog?" He moved toward Buffy, Annie's longtime companion and the shop's mascot.

Annie retrieved a large pink box from the stack and began filling it. "Not really. She just likes to come with me." Annie taped the box shut.

"I like dogs." He leaned over and patted Buffy on the head.

"She likes people." She reached for the second box.

"I don't have any pets right now, but I hope to have a dog someday." The handsome man's smile made her pulse race.

"Cash or card?" she asked, biting down a smile, the beating of her heart quickening by the minute.

"Cash." The man pulled out a black leather wallet from the inside of his suit jacket. He handed Annie a hundred-dollar bill. She quickly made his change and watched as he put his wallet away. The man bobbled the boxes as he slid one hand out from under the bottom. "Jack Powell."

Annie brushed her hand across her apron. "Annie McPherson."

"I'm sort of sorry I haven't stopped in here before today." His eyes twinkled.

"Well, the important thing is that you finally did." Her bottom lip quivered just a bit.

"Thanks again for the cupcakes. I'm sure my niece and all her friends will devour them." He took the boxes and headed toward the shop's door.

Annie watched his medium-sized frame, large shoulders, and muscular thighs move as he crossed to the door. She kept her gaze steady on him—just in case he turned around quickly and caught her drooling ... staring.

"Oh, by the way," he said, twirling around and smiling as he did. "You have a little flour above your top lip."

She quickly rubbed her face with her fingertips. "Thanks," she whispered.

Annie didn't typically get so flustered with

customers, but this Jack Powell fellow had her not only turning a few shades of red, but had her tummy tied up in knots as well.

~

A different day, but the same routine brought Annie into the bakery. Annie really liked to bake. It helped her de-stress, especially when it came to her meddling grandmother and auntie with their insistence to find her a man. She began to hum a tune that her mom used to sing to her when she heard the door open.

Annie looked up from the counter, locking eyes once again with Jack Powell. "I thought you were Morgan. She just left."

"Morgan?"

"My helper. She comes in a few hours a week to help me bake."

"I see. Well, are you disappointed that I'm not Morgan?" Jack lowered his head, his eyes trying to grab her gaze.

She paused a moment before answering. "No, not at all. How many cupcakes do you want today?" She turned toward the stacked pink boxes and retrieved one.

"Just one," he replied.

Annie hesitated before placing the box back. She turned slowly. "One cupcake? What flavor?" She pulled out a piece of the dry waxed paper and placed it on the counter.

"Carrot, and a small cup of coffee, too." He turned toward the small pub-style table. "I'll eat it here."

"I don't serve coffee."

"No coffee? Gotta have coffee with sweets. You should add that to your menu."

Annie opened the display case and retrieved his cupcake. "I think having coffee is a great idea," she said as she plopped the cupcake down on a paper plate. "That'll be two dollars, please." Annie smiled.

Jack handed her two bucks, took his cupcake, and crossed over to the tall table in the corner. He casually glanced back toward her.

Annie tried not to be obvious as she watched him put the scrumptious treat to his mouth. He leaned back in the chair, enjoying the sugary delight when he suddenly turned around, holding the cupcake up. "Tasty," he said. "Sure would taste a whole lot better with a cup of coffee."

Annie slipped into the kitchen in the back. She didn't want to advertise it, but she had a Keurig coffee maker.

She put the cup of steaming coffee down in front of him. "Cream or sugar?"

He lowered his head and stared into the cup. "I thought you didn't have coffee?" A surprised look crossed his face as he lifted the cup, inhaling the brew.

"I don't. Not for paying customers. But, I agree, I like coffee with my sweets, too. I have a personal coffee maker in the kitchen." A wide smile appeared on her face.

"Well, in that case, cream and sugar."

Annie headed back to the kitchen to get the cream and sugar. She'd just reached the threshold between the kitchen and the display case, armed with the cream and sugar when he called out, "Grab a cup and join me."

She stopped, took a few steps back, and grabbed her cup with her index finger. Balancing the cream, sugar, and now her ceramic cup, she traveled over to where he sat. She liked how this day was shaping up.

Over coffee, Jack and Annie made small talk. In about fifteen minutes, she found he'd lived in the Charleston area his entire life and his whole family lived in the vicinity.

She told him her story. Well, not all of it. She'd save some of it for later. Not everyone would be receptive to her meddling grandmother and auntie. They meant well and over time, Annie had learned how to handle them. Or had she?

"Why cupcakes?" he asked as he took his last bite of the carrot cake with cream cheese frosting.

"One night, the girls and I were sitting around, drinking our sorrows away in a bottle of great zinfandel when we got hungry for sweets. I had some chocolate cupcakes leftover from one of the girl's bridal shower, and before we knew it, Sweet Indulgence was born."

"Were these cupcakes you'd baked?" He drew in a sip of his coffee.

"Yes. I've always enjoyed baking. I make a mean chocolate chip and oatmeal cookie, too."

"And then finding the best place to sell your cupcakes …" He trailed off, waiting for her to pick up on the conversation.

She swallowed her sip of coffee and nodded. "This is the perfect location. We're close to all the action — shops, dining. I couldn't have asked for a better location."

"Do you live around here?"

"Yes, about two blocks from here. I have an apartment above the cigar shop on Anne Avenue."

"You live on Anne Avenue. How cute."

She laughed. "I thought it was a sign. My real name is Anne, but my friends call me Annie."

Jack glanced at his watch. "Oh, man, I have to be going. Where did the time go?" He slid back his chair and stood. "I have a client to pick up in about fifteen minutes." He crossed over toward the door and opened it.

"No problem. Thanks for coming back. Maybe I'll see you again sometime." She relaxed her face and the corners of her mouth drew up.

Jack nodded. "You can count on it."

CHAPTER 2

*a*nnie sat at the kitchen table going over last month's accounts receivable and expenses. She leaned back into the chair and casually turned her head. With her paws flicking, nose twitching, and the occasional whimper as she chased bunnies in her dream, Buffy gave Annie a welcomed distraction from business.

She pushed her chair back and stood, crossing to the large window with a view of the street below. The narrow cobblestone road, a part of Charleston's history dating to the 1800s, gave Annie a reason to sigh. And sigh she did. "It's a beautiful day for a walk, Buffy," she said, turning around.

Buffy's chocolate brown eyes blinked a couple of times along with her thumping tail. "You're awake! Go get your leash," Annie said. The little dog jumped up and ran over to her hanging leash and nudged it with her nose. Annie laughed. "That's a good girl."

They headed down to the Waterfront Park. Like most days, loads of people were wandering around. She found an empty bench and sat down, her eyes drifting to the pier where people were lined up along one side and down the other as they looked off into the Harbor. Buffy tugged at her leash causing Annie to look down.

"Leave it!" Annie jumped up and kicked the rotten piece of fruit out of her reach. "Seriously, Buffy. Must you be such a chowhound?" Annie coaxed her to walk, trying to get her away from the spoiled food.

They walked past a couple with a young child. She already sensed the child would ask her if she could pet her dog. It happened at least once a day on their walks.

"Can I pet your dog?" the cute little girl with blonde ringlets asked.

"Sure." Annie smiled.

The little girl gently patted Buffy's head and then moved her hand along her back. "She's a nice little doggy."

"Yes, she is. She comes to work with me every day. She loves people," Annie said.

The little girl's mother tilted her head. "Oh? Where do you work at?"

"I own Sweet Indulgence Cupcakery." Annie puffed out her chest.

"Oh, we walked by there today, but it was closed," the mother replied.

"I'm only open until two o'clock. I hope to expand my hours soon. I'm basically a one man ... err, woman, show right now. I do have a college student who helps me out a few hours a week. And I'm happy to say, I should be able to give her more hours soon."

The mother of the little girl nodded. "Well, this little one is having a birthday next month. I'll stop by and order some cupcakes for the big day." The mother smiled lovingly at her daughter who now was tugging at her blouse. "Can we get a dog?" she pleaded.

"Honey, we've been over that before. We can't right now." The mother turned to Annie. "We live in an apartment."

"I totally understand. I don't have a yard either, but thankfully, I live near this beautiful park," Annie said, motioning with her hands the grassy area that Buffy frequented.

"Do you have a business card with the bakery's number?"

Annie frowned. "Wait, I think I do." She dug into her purse and retrieved a crumpled looking piece of cardboard. "I'm sorry about its condition. It's been riding around in my purse. It's on my to-do list to order more."

"Thank you. This works," the mother said.

"Well, we're going to walk the pier before we head home. Have a nice day." Annie tugged at Buffy's leash, but Buffy didn't budge. "Buffy, come on." Annie tugged her leash again. Buffy reluctantly moved away from the little girl's soft touches.

"Bye," the little girl said as she waved goodbye to the little dog.

Annie nodded and smiled and then proceeded to the pier. A lot of things traveled through her mind regarding the cupcakery. It excited her beyond control how a little idea had grown into a full-time business and something like walking Buffy just got her more customers. Her folks would be so proud. Her eyes began to fill with tears. It never got any easier. She missed them every day.

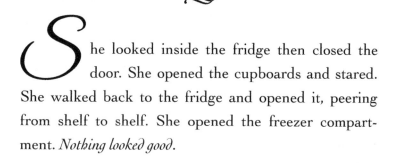

*S*he looked inside the fridge then closed the door. She opened the cupboards and stared. She walked back to the fridge and opened it, peering from shelf to shelf. She opened the freezer compartment. *Nothing looked good.*

She fed Buffy and then grabbed a light sweater. "I'll be back in about an hour," she said as she patted her head.

Annie strolled down the sidewalk about three blocks to one of her favorite seafood restaurants. *Shrimp and Grits. Now that sounded good!*

The hostess led the way to a small table in a corner near a window. Annie loved to people watch so this was perfect. The hostess left a menu with her. She didn't have the heart to tell her she already knew what she wanted. Soon the waitress came over to take her drink order.

"Iced tea and shrimp and grits," Annie said, handing her the menu.

The brunette giggled. "You already know what you want to eat, too."

"I didn't know for sure until I was about here, but then my mouth began to water for your shrimp and grits."

"It's one of my favorites, too," a man's voice said from behind her.

Annie reeled her neck around to find Jack sitting there. "How'd I walk by you and not see you?" Annie asked.

"I probably had my nose in the menu." He looked

up at the waitress who hadn't moved yet. "May I join you?"

"Sure, please do."

"I'll have what she's having." Jack handed the waitress the menu.

"I'll be right back with your drinks," the waitress announced with a southern drawl.

Jack plopped down in the chair opposite of Annie. Annie lowered her gaze to the silverware and began to rearrange it. She felt a bit uneasy about Jack sitting right across from her although she liked the idea a few moments before.

"Funny meeting you here." He picked up a fork and played with it.

Annie realized they both were fingering the utensils. "I think I'm nervous for some reason."

"Why? Do I make you nervous?" Jack asked.

"I think so. I'm not sure why, though." Annie locked her eyes on him. He was more gorgeous than she remembered, with his dark hair, dark eyes, and bronze complexion.

"Would you like to order anything from the bar?" the waitress asked as she set the glasses of iced tea on the table.

Jack turned to Annie and shrugged. "A glass of wine, perhaps?"

"Wine sounds good," Annie echoed.

"Two glasses of cabernet sauvignon." Jack turned his attention back to Annie. "With a name like Annie McPherson, I imagine your ancestors came from Ireland."

Annie flashed him a wide smile. "Yes, in fact, I just did a DNA test and got back my results."

"Let me guess. You were surprised when it came back you were Irish?" He winked, making her blush.

"Well," she said, "It just so happens that I am not just Irish. I'm twenty percent British, thirty percent Eastern European, and the rest is Irish." She drew in a long drink of her iced tea.

The waitress brought them their wine and left quietly.

"Were your parents able to help you with some of the connections?"

Annie shook her head. "My parents are gone. My mom died when I was ten, and my dad died about five years ago in a car accident."

"Any brothers or sisters?"

"Yes, Mary my younger sister. She's off traveling Europe with her friends. A graduation present from my grandmother and auntie."

Jack cleared his throat. "I have a sister, Diane. She's

older by a few years. Her husband, my brother-in-law, Richard also works for the company."

"They must be the parents of your birthday girl?"

"Yes, Crystal."

"And your folks?"

"I have my mom and dad, both sets of grandparents, three uncles and their wives, and several cousins. We have a huge family."

Annie relaxed her shoulders and dropped her gaze.

"Hey, I didn't make you sad, did I?"

Annie shrugged. "A little. I always wished I had more brothers and sisters. The holidays are the worst."

"Well, you can come to my house whenever you want loud and obnoxious. You'll get your fill of family life pretty quickly." He smiled, and instantly she felt better.

"You have beautiful skin," Annie said, changing the subject.

Jack studied his forearm as he rolled it back and forth. "Indian blood."

"Oh? How fascinating," Annie said.

"My great-great-grandmother belonged to the Kiawah tribe."

"I love the Kiawah River area," Annie stated cheerfully.

"You probably lather on the sunscreen?" He laughed.

"Guilty, but I do love the warmth of the sun. I just have to be careful how long I stay in it."

"That green blouse plays up your pretty eyes." He put the wine glass to his lips.

"Thank you," she whispered.

Annie caught a glimpse of the waitress carrying a wooden serving tray. In her free hand, she balanced the round serving tray that held their dinners. She placed the white dish in front of Annie. The wonderful smells drifted upward.

"And for you, sir," she said, setting down the second plate. "Be careful it's hot. Enjoy your dinner."

They dined on the shrimp and grits, and in between bites, got more acquainted and learned that they both had a few things in common besides loving sugar.

"One of these days I'd love to take you out on my boat."

Jack focused on her mouth, making her squirm a bit. His sexiness working its way into her and making her feel anxious. She shook her head, trying to clear the uncertainty of what might be playing out before her.

"No? You wouldn't want to ride on my boat?" He cocked his head to the left.

"No, I didn't mean that. I was just thinking about

something else. Of course, a boat ride sounds delightful." She took a bite of the grits covered in a rich, savory gravy.

"How about Saturday?" His excitement bursting at the seams caused her to giggle.

"Saturdays are busy for me at the bakery."

"Of course, I should have thought of that. Let's see, how about Friday? I can take the afternoon off. The boat isn't far from here. I could pick you up at around noon."

Annie drew in a big breath, exhaling quickly. Her heart was pumping fast and hard. "Okay. I usually close up by two o'clock. Let me see if Morgan can stay and close up. It really depends on her schedule."

"You're going to need to hire more people soon."

Annie tilted her head. "Oh, why?"

Jack chuckled. "Those cupcakes are the best I've ever had. My niece's birthday party was a hit because of them. You wait. Your doors will be swinging back and forth nonstop pretty soon." He winked, and Annie could feel herself blush.

She reached up and pulled her hair back, straightening her shoulders. "I see. You can tell the future, can you?" She smiled.

"I can't eat another bite. I'm stuffed." He pushed his plate to the side.

"No dessert, then." She smiled coyly.

"I already had mine today at Sweet Indulgence, with you."

She nodded. "True."

The waitress brought the check, and before Annie could get a look at it, Jack took his wallet out, handing her his credit card. "All of it on me." He winked.

"Thank you, Jack. I didn't expect that."

"I know you didn't. That's what makes it so nice." He reached across the table and patted her hand that had been resting on the table. She slowly drew it back.

"It's getting late. I should be going."

"Let me walk you home."

A typical spring evening, the warm air had people out and about, and the sounds of chatter echoed the streets. It would have been totally safe for her to walk home alone. She did it all the time, but it was nice to have Jack by her side.

"Here we are." Annie stopped in front of the cigar shop.

Jack gazed upward. "Is your apartment up there?"

Annie took a few more steps, which brought them to the corner where the cobblestone alley was located. She motioned with her chin down the alley. "My door is down there."

Jack extended his arm out. "After you," he said, having her take the lead.

"Here we are." Annie pulled out her key and put it in the lock. She turned and gazed at him over her shoulder. "Thanks again for dinner and for walking me home. I had a great time."

"I mean it about the boat ride." He reached into his pocket, drew out a card, and handed it to her. "My cell number is on here. Please call. It should be a nice day out on the inlet."

Turning to face him she said, "Okay, I'll try to work it out."

"Fair enough." He reached his hand out, resting it on her arm.

His touch sent a wave of emotions running through her body, causing the hair on her arms to stand. She pulled up her shoulders and trembled. "Good night, Jack."

She shut the door and climbed the several steps that led up to her apartment. She unlocked the second door and entered the living room where Buffy waited patiently, wagging her tail. Annie tossed her purse onto the table and leaned over, petting her on the head. "You won't believe who I ran into." She brushed her hand down Buffy's ears and scratched the inside, causing Buffy to itch her hind end with her back feet. Annie laughed. "Yup, Jack, and boy did he look handsome tonight. He even paid for my dinner." Buffy followed her into the bedroom.

She took out the business card he'd handed her and started to toss it on the dresser when something caught her eye.

Jack Powell – Driver

Powell Limousine Services

She read the card again as the words sank in. *He was a chauffeur?*

Her mind raced back to their conversation over cupcakes and coffee. He never really mentioned what he did for a living nor did she ask. So what if he was a chauffeur or a professional driver. It was honest work and who said it always has to be about the money? Annie gasped. Grandmother Lilly—that's who.

CHAPTER 3

"*Hi*. I think I can manage that boat ride," she whispered. It'd only taken her an hour to get the nerve to dial his number.

"Great. You made my day. I don't get a lot of days off either, but my family is stepping in today for me. I'll pick you up at around noon."

"That's great. Hey, so … you're a limo driver?" She might as well get it out in the open. You know, just so she could come up with a story if the time ever came. For Grandmother Lilly, she told herself.

"Yup, well, mostly. I drive, my brother-in-law drives, and my dad occasionally drives when he wants to get away from my mother," he said. "And during peak times, we have other family members help out when they can."

"Oh, that's great. Charleston is visited by many so I'm sure you keep busy."

"My sister Diane runs the vacation rentals, and Mom helps by decorating them and all that nonsense."

"Oh, you have quite a setup, then, not just a transportation service." A smile crossed her face. This would be much easier to sell to Grandmother.

~

*A*nnie smiled at the beautiful scenery as they drove to the dock where Jack's boat was moored. She had her bathing suit on under a cover-up. She grabbed her beach bag and followed him down the pier, her flip-flops slapping the wooden planks.

"Here she is." He smiled as he pointed.

"She's beautiful. What's her name?"

"She's in between names right now." He jumped in the boat and held out his hand.

Annie took his hand and lowered herself into the boat. He leaned over the side and untied the one rope that held her securely to the dock, and soon they were on their way, motoring quietly and slowly at first, then opening up wide and hard as they rode the open waters. Annie sat in the back, but after several minutes of sea spray slapping her in the face and her hair whipping in the wind, she moved toward the open seat up front near him and under the protection of the canopy.

"I think I got enough sun." She smoothed her hand over her fair arms.

"Be careful. You can really get burned out here and not know it. I have refreshments in the cooler. Help yourself."

Annie retrieved two bottles of ice cold water. She handed Jack one. "Why is the boat in between names?" She took a sip of the water. It felt great on her parched lips, and the cool water quenched her dry throat.

"That's a long story." He peered out into the water before them.

She took another gulp of water. It really tasted good. He was right. The heat could really sneak up on you when you're riding in a boat.

"Well, we have time for long stories, don't we?" She batted her lashes. She wasn't letting him off the hook that easy.

"I had a girlfriend."

"You named your boat after a girlfriend?" Annie frowned.

"She was more than a girlfriend. We were engaged to be married." His eyes never left the water.

"A fiancée, we call people we are engaged to be married to fiancés." She giggled.

He turned quickly with furrowed brows then he resumed with eyes steady on the water.

"I'm kidding." She touched his arm and withdrew it quickly. "Anyway, you named the boat after your fiancée and now you two are no longer a couple, so the boat is nameless," Annie spoke freely.

"That's about the size of it."

"How about you give the boat a name that means something to you that would never change?"

Jack looked back over his shoulder and then turned back around toward the front of the boat. All of a sudden, he cut the engine and they began to drift. He turned and sat down, bringing his bottle of water to his lips and drew in a drink. "I thought about that. But I'm terrible at naming things."

"Let's see. I named my dog Buffy because of her color." Annie searched the boat with her eyes for clues. "How about *Lady Luck*?"

"I've seen a few named that. I want something more original."

Annie lowered her gaze and stared at her bright pink toe polish. She raised her head quickly. "I know. How about *Lady Powell*?"

Jack snapped his fingers. "I like that." He laughed. "Hey, are you getting hungry?"

"Getting there."

"I brought sandwiches from the deli. I know of a place we can tie the boat and have lunch."

"Sounds great, Jack."

He put the boat in gear and headed toward their destination. She had no idea where he was taking her. They'd only motored for about fifteen more minutes when he dropped back the speed. In the distance she saw a boat dock.

Jack pushed up the throttle, and the boat idled as he drifted to the spot he wanted. He cut the motor off and jumped out of the boat, grabbing the coiled rope on the deck. "I know it looks bad, but it's safe. I've reinforced the planks a few times, especially after hurricanes." Jack stood on the pier and helped Annie out.

"What is this, some private island?" Annie asked.

"Sort of."

Annie stood on the dock and looked around, trying to get her bearings. "Is this Kiawah?"

"Yes, it is. Remember I told you my great-great-grandmother was from the Kiawah Indians? Well, legend has it that her ancestors lived on this land. It was near water for growing crops and to drink, and it was beautiful." Jack looked off into the distance.

"You can say that again. It's absolutely gorgeous out here. So peaceful."

"When my mom's grandparents passed away, my grandparents inherited the land."

"You're very lucky, Jack."

He tilted his head. "Why do you say that?"

"Not only do you have a family, but you have history and this beautiful parcel."

They made their way to solid ground, and soon a picnic table came into view. The weather-beaten benches and table had seen better days, too. Jack brushed off twigs and other things that had fallen on the benches and top. He tossed the soft bag he'd retrieved from the cooler on top. He unzipped the thermal bag and handed her the white deli paper wrapped sandwich. "I hope you like turkey."

"I do. I like food, period." She laughed.

Annie turned her head and began searching the area with her eyes. She saw movement out of the corner of her eye and focused. It was a squirrel. She looked up at the huge branches of the oak tree draped in moss that gave their table shade.

"So many beautiful oaks." She took a bite of her sandwich.

"Yes, and we have some dogwoods further back and the grandmother or daddy of all trees, a beautiful magnolia. After lunch, we can explore."

Annie swallowed her bite down and took a sip of her water.

The two explored the entire area. The lot his family owned was a slice of paradise, also known as Kiawah Island. A barrier island known for beautiful beaches, golf courses, and resorts, its proximity to Charleston made it a perfect getaway for locals and attracted tourists by the thousands.

"This little one-way bridge makes it feel like we are a separate island from the mainland," Jack said as they strolled over the weather-beaten wooden bridge.

"I love it. The marsh is so pretty this time of year," Annie said, pointing to the wispy reeds and the snowy white egrets that probed the muddy waters of the wetlands. "It's like your own little piece of heaven."

"We used to camp out here when we were teens. We had a blast," Jack said as he reminisced.

"It wasn't scary? It's pretty dark out here at night," Annie said.

"We had flashlights and lanterns. And we also had a fire going down at the beach."

"I know … right … your own private beach," Annie said smiling. "This would be a beautiful spot to build a home on. Why haven't you built on it?"

"Well …"

Annie realized quickly what she'd stepped into. "It's

the fiancée, isn't it? I'm sorry, really I am. I shouldn't have said anything."

He reached his arms, out placing one hand on each of her arms. "No, it's okay. I have to start talking about it eventually. Yes. My grandparents were giving us this as a wedding present. I was going to build a house on it." He turned his head and looked over his shoulder slightly. When he turned back around to face Annie, she swore she saw moisture in his eyes.

She swallowed hard. "Listen, I know what it's like having a broken heart. It doesn't matter if it's a boyfriend, girlfriend, parents or whomever."

He removed his hands from her arms and laced his fingers of one with hers, gently squeezing her hand. She could feel the blood run straight to her cheeks. She drew in her bottom lip between her teeth.

"I say I'm over her, and sometimes I really am. Then I see her with her new guy laughing and kissing him, and it brings the memories back." He lowered his head.

She sighed. "I know, memories can be brutal. I have a few of my own to deal with as well."

He jerked his head up, searching her eyes for answers. "What do you mean?"

"Let's save that for the next boat ride and picnic, shall we?"

CHAPTER 4

"*B*ut, Grandmother Lilly, I don't want to go on another date that you've set up. All of yours and Auntie Patty's have been major disasters. I met a guy I'd like you to meet. His name is Jack." Annie held out the phone from her ear as she heard Grandmother Lilly chattering about how it was their responsibility to help her find a good man.

"You two need a hobby—ceramics, painting, anything but me." Annie could feel her blood boiling, her Irish blood.

"Oh, child, don't be silly. We're very busy. We play cards once a week, we attend charity events and church. Don't forget our participation at Our Lady of the Lake Church."

"Well, it's apparently not enough to keep you busy because you both insist on making my life a—"

"Be careful, Annie. You can't take it back once you say it," Lilly said with a tone of warning.

"Oh, Grandmother! I just want to find my own dates."

"You've had three broken hearts within the last eighteen months. You clearly are choosing the wrong type of men."

"That's not true." Annie didn't want to admit that maybe it was.

"And, because you're so resistant to our choices, you'll never know if we even came close to selecting the right mate for you."

"Selecting the right mate? Do you hear yourself talking? This is not the days of arranged marriages. I'm free to pick my own guy, failure or not," Annie said, raising her voice a tad.

"There's more involved here than just your failures, Annie. You are to inherit a lot of money someday. Your future husband must not be a money-grubbing individual and must be able to hold his own in terms of financial success."

"Okay, now you just sound paranoid. I can't talk to you about this any longer. I'll be over for dinner tonight. See you then." She lowered her head in defeat.

She looked over to find Buffy staring up at her with big brown eyes. "They'll never leave me alone until I marry the man of their dreams."

$\sim$

*I*t always started out nice. The table would be set with the finest china and silverware. They would serve only the best food and wine and then they would go in for the kill, with her grandmother on one side and Auntie Patty on the other. Resisting these two old women proved to be impossible, and after an hour of badgering, she agreed she'd go out to dinner with Chad, Mrs. Palmdale's nephew.

"Thank you, dear. You are going to just love Chad. He's such a gentleman. He is an attorney," Grandmother Lilly said, nodding her head toward Auntie Patty.

Annie chewed her pork tenderloin long past its tenderness, trying to stall. She drew in a drink of water to help wash down the meat, and then stabbed the green beans with her fork like a three-year old.

"Aren't you going to say anything?" Auntie Patty asked.

Annie put her fork down and clasped her hands, pushing the plate aside. "And say what? You two seem to have already decided my future. Who I'll date, probably who I'll marry, and most definitely what I name my first child." She frowned at them both.

Grandmother Lilly sputtered and Auntie Patty sighed loudly.

"That's ridiculous. We let you run your own business and live on your own, even though we know your dad would have wanted you to live with us." Grandmother Lilly drew in a taste of her wine from her second, or was it her third glass? Annie had stopped counting. Grandmother Lilly loved her wine. And then there was Auntie Patty's choice of adult beverage — scotch with a splash of water.

"Mary lives with you. You wouldn't have room for me, too. Besides, I have Buffy, and you are allergic to dogs." Annie pushed her chair back, her still clasped hands now lying in her lap.

"Just give Chad a try. He really is a nice guy," Auntie Patty pleaded.

Annie drew in a deep breath. It was of no use. These old women ruled the roost. Man, she wished her dad was here. She really missed him. "I make no promises." Annie stood.

"I'll make a promise to you," Grandmother Lilly said.

Under half closed lids, Annie listened on.

"If Chad doesn't work out, we'll stop meddling."

Annie deepened her furrow. "Seriously? What's the catch?"

"No catch. I discussed with Patty your concerns, and we're in agreement that you should be able to choose your own mate. Failure is just part of life."

"Oh, Grandmother Lilly, thank you. I'm so happy to hear you say that."

Grandmother slid her chair back and stood. "So keep us posted."

Annie already had ideas how to end the date before it even started. They'd never be the wiser. "I will."

"Time for my pills. If you'll excuse me." Grandmother hobbled out of sight.

Annie sat at the table with Auntie Patty, thinking about the conversation the three of them had. She looked over at Auntie Patty and smiled.

"Don't be fooled for a second that your grandmother did that out of the kindness of her heart."

Annie knitted her brows together. "What do you mean?"

"She knows Mary will be home soon. She's going to drive her crazy with the blind dates. You watch." Patty took a sip of her drink.

Annie sighed, heaving her shoulders up and down. "Well, all I can say is she better be careful. Mary is nothing like me. She's so strong-willed and determined, she'll probably run off and get married to the worst sleazebag in the world if you guys mess with her."

Patty turned to Annie. "Don't sell yourself short. You're one of the most determined women I know. You just approach it differently than Mary does."

Annie slid her chair back and came to Patty's side. "Thanks for saying that. I love you." She gave Patty a quick kiss on the cheek.

"What am I? Chicken liver?"

Annie looked up to find Grandmother standing in the doorway to the dining room. "Of course not. I love you, too." Annie moved to where her grandmother stood and wrapped her arms around her, hugging her tightly. "I must be going. I have an early day."

"Oh, Annie?" Grandmother Lilly called out.

Annie let out a sigh as she turned around, placing her hands on her hips. "What now?"

"Calm down, child. I was just going to ask you if you'd heard from Mary." Grandmother Lilly squinted her eyes as she scowled at Annie.

"No. No, I haven't. I imagine she's having the time of her life somewhere in Paris, or maybe Barcelona." Annie recalled her recent conversation with Auntie Patty about Mary.

Grandmother Lilly nodded. "I just worry about her. When is she due back?"

Annie glanced at her watch. "Hmm. I think she returns on the twenty-fourth, but I'll double-check. I'm picking her up at the airport."

"Keep us posted, dear. We love you girls."

"Yes, Grandmother." Annie relaxed her stance. "Try to stay out of trouble, you two." She winked.

~

*A*nnie finished baking all the cupcakes before her regular deadline. She'd just taken off her apron when the door swung open. It was Jack.

She pulled her eyebrows in and pursed her lips. "Hey, I wasn't expecting you."

"I know. I couldn't help but think about you in that green bikini." He winked at her causing her to fidget.

"Oh, you noticed, did you?" She lowered her eyes to the floor.

"I wanted to know if you were free later today. I wanted to take you on a drive."

Annie poked her head up and locked gazes with him. *That's right, he was a professional driver. Of course, he'd like to drive.*

"I wish I could, but my grandmother and auntie have set me up on another blind date."

"Oh, I see." He ran his hand across his chin.

Annie spoke fast. "It's not like that. It's not serious at all. It never is, except for them. They are constantly trying to set me up with men they feel will be my soul mate. They don't think I have a mind of my own."

"Okay, another time, then." Jack took a few steps backward toward the front door.

She couldn't let him leave thinking the date was any more than her meddling relatives' idea of entertainment.

"I'd like that, Jack, I really would. Can I get a rain check?" she said, her lips parting slightly and her limbs tingling with anticipation.

He gave her a back wave. "Sure, I'll get back to you."

She watched him as he exited the shop, his head hanging down. She'd disappointed him. *No ... Grandmother and Auntie had!*

CHAPTER 5

*J*ust as she'd predicted, the date with Chad was anything but memorable. Well, except for the fact that she had to listen to him talk about himself endlessly, the entire time with spinach stuck in his teeth.

"Okay, so it didn't work out with Chad," Grandmother Lilly said over tea and scones.

"He wasn't interested in me at all," Annie said exaggeratingly.

"A promise is a promise. No more dates, no more setups. You're free to make your own choices." Lilly raised her chin, pointing her nose upward.

"It's all good. We are going to remain friends," Annie said, trying to smooth things over.

"There's always Mary. She'll need some help in

finding a nice young man," Grandmother said under her breath.

Annie had already got wind of this harebrained idea from Auntie Patty. "Haven't you learned your lesson? I know you keep spouting about how you're doing this for Mom and Dad, and you have to protect our interest, and all of that baloney, but to tell you the truth, all you're really doing is putting a wedge between all of us."

Maybe she'd said too much. Now both women were picking up their hankies and dabbing their eyes. "I didn't mean to upset you. It's just I'm tired of all the set ups. They always end in disaster, a waste of an evening for me, and...I just want to find my own dates."

Grandmother sniffled back her fake tears. While Auntie looked on.

"Okay, I'll tell you what. Bring Jerry—" Auntie said, always the peace keeper.

"Jack!" Annie interrupted.

"Oh, yes, Jack ... bring him over for tea." Auntie Patty twisted her mouth as she looked over to Grandmother Lilly for approval. "Lilly," Auntie Patty shouted.

"Oh, okay, bring him over, but I probably won't like him," Grandmother grumbled.

"How can you even say that without meeting him?"

"What did you say he did for employment?" Auntie Patty asked.

Annie wasn't prepared for this line of questioning, not just yet. She pulled her hair back off her shoulders and straightened her back. She glanced at her watch as she said, "I must be going. I'll let you know when he can come."

Annie moved across the living room toward the long hall that led to the front door. She could hear the shuffling of feet with the sound of canes tapping as they followed behind. She reached for the doorknob, and as she turned the knob, feeling the freedom of her exit, Grandmother Lilly called out.

"You didn't answer. What does Jackson do for a living?"

Annie whirled around. "His name is Jack. Just Jack. And I didn't say what he did for a living."

Grandmother Lilly glanced quickly over to Patty and then back to Annie.

"Don't worry. He has an honorable position with a family business. It's been around for years. Have a great afternoon." Annie took off down the steps and down the walk that would lead her to her car. She sat in the driver's seat, breathing heavily. She slammed her head back onto the headrest, staring at the car's headliner. She shook her head slowly. "Those old women are going to plan my entire life if I don't get a handle on things now." She started the engine and zoomed down the road, not caring about the thirty-five miles per hour speed limit until she saw the black and white car positioned on the corner. She pumped the brakes a couple of times, slowing down the car, and then stopped at the stop sign. She looked over at the officer and smiled and then proceeded to drive home.

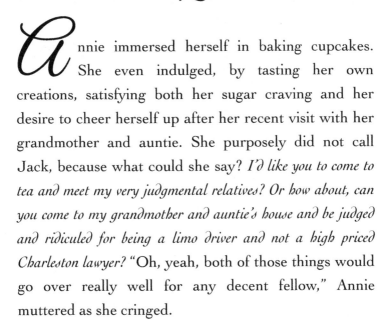

*A*nnie immersed herself in baking cupcakes. She even indulged, by tasting her own creations, satisfying both her sugar craving and her desire to cheer herself up after her recent visit with her grandmother and auntie. She purposely did not call Jack, because what could she say? *I'd like you to come to tea and meet my very judgmental relatives? Or how about, can you come to my grandmother and auntie's house and be judged and ridiculed for being a limo driver and not a high priced Charleston lawyer?* "Oh, yeah, both of those things would go over really well for any decent fellow," Annie muttered as she cringed.

Annie looked up when she heard the bakery door open. In dashed Morgan. "Hello," Annie called out as Morgan brushed by her.

"Sorry, I'm late." She grabbed an apron off the hook.

"No worries, but I did want to speak to you." Annie lined up the cupcakes row by row.

"I'm really sorry for being late," Morgan repeated.

"I know, you said that already. I wanted to ask you about working extra hours. I went over the books. We're making a profit each month — a substantial one. Now, I know you can't work a lot more with your school schedule, but even if you could give me just four more hours, I'd be grateful."

Morgan tied the apron around her waist. "I think I can handle that. When were you thinking?"

"Oh, that's great. Well, right now, you're coming in on Mondays, Wednesdays, Fridays, and Saturdays for two hours each day. I'd like to increase Saturdays to six hours, since I seem to be busiest on weekends and you won't be in classes. You can pick which other days work best for you for any additional hours you might be able to work."

"Okay, Annie, let me double-check a few things, but I think that'll work just fine." Morgan crossed into the kitchen to retrieve a pan of baked cupcakes. "What icing do you want me to make?" she called out.

"Salted caramel," Annie shouted back. "It's the favorite again this week."

~

"*I* haven't heard from you in a few days. Is everything all right?" Jack asked.

Annie paused before answering, happy they were speaking on the phone and not in person. "Yes, I've just been swamped at the bakery. I even increased Morgan's hours." That wasn't a lie.

"That's great, Annie. I'm happy for you. I think you have the perfect business for our area."

Annie walked into her living room and plopped down on her sofa, resting her feet on the glass coffee table. She leaned back into the sofa cushions. "I wanted to ask you something. Feel free to say no."

"Okay." Jack chuckled.

"My grandmother and auntie would like to meet you. Are you up for tea?"

"Tea? Seriously? You mean with china cups and saucers?" Jack asked.

"I'm afraid so," Annie whispered.

"Well, I guess so. If it's that important to you."

"It's just that they are always setting me up with their friends' grandsons or nephews and I'm tired of it all. The last date was another disaster among a long line of disasters. I just thought if they met you they'd leave me alone."

"What have you told them about me?" Jack asked.

"Nothing, really. Just your name."

"Ahh, okay. Let me ask you this. What do you want them to know about me?"

"Just your name." Annie laughed when she recalled them getting his name wrong.

"If your grandmother and auntie are anything like mine, they are going to grill me for more than my name."

~

"Now, remember, they are going to call you everything but Jack. Don't take it as they don't like you. It's just who they are," Annie said, already making excuses for them.

"You mean a bit on the snobbish side?" Jack ran his hand through his hair and then straightened his shirt.

"Are you nervous?" Annie asked.

"A little bit. I feel a bit like I'm walking into a lion's den." He peered at her through half closed lids.

Annie lowered her gaze.

"I am. I'm walking into a lion's den, right?" Jack frowned.

"Just follow my lead, and everything will be fine." Annie tapped on the front door with the brass knocker.

The sounds of leather soles on wood floors and low mumblings from the old women gave clue they were approaching the door. "Here they come, breathe."

"Good day, dear." Grandmother Lilly opened the door wide.

"Grandmother, this is Jack."

Grandmother Lilly's eyes widened as she took the young man in by the hand. "It's so nice to meet you, ahh …"

"Jack," Annie prompted.

"Why, yes, Jack. Please come in."

Annie raised her brows as she focused on Jack's eyes. "Sorry," she whispered.

Auntie Patty stood in the doorway that led to the formal living room. She took a few steps back so the group could enter the room.

"Auntie Patty, this is Jack," Annie said.

She extended her hand to Jack. "You can call me Patty."

Annie led Jack to the Queen Anne style sofa while Grandmother Lilly and Auntie Patty each sat in a high-backed chair. Annie saw the china tea service sitting on the tea table nearby.

"Be a dear and pour us some tea," Grandmother Lilly said.

Annie jumped up to pour the tea, trying to keep an

ear on the conversation. She heard her grandmother ask him about his parents.

"Here we go. One for you, and one for you," Annie said as she handed her grandmother and then her auntie each a cup. "Jack, what do you like in your tea?"

"Cream and sugar, please."

Annie hurried over to the tea service and poured their cups. She plopped down next to him, handing him his cup. She smiled at him quickly, putting her hand up to stop her quivering lips. "Jack's family has lived in Charleston for ages. Isn't that right, Jack?" Annie drew in a sip of her tea.

"Yes. My great-great grandmother was from the Kiawah tribe. My family is deeply rooted here in Charleston."

"How nice," Grandmother Lilly said.

"Our family has lived in Charleston for generations, too. This house was built in the 1800s and has been handed down ever since. It will be Annie's someday." Auntie Patty smiled.

"It's a beautiful house." Jack glanced around the very ornately furnished room.

"Yes, it is. Our parents lived here and before them, well …" Patty trailed off.

"After our husbands died, we decided to live

together. It's worked out rather well, don't you think, Patty?" Lilly asked.

"Yes, indeed. We are sisters." Patty stiffened her back and lifted her chin.

"What do you do for a living?" Lilly asked.

"Grandmother, that's not really important, is it?" Annie asked, trying to shield Jack from the twenty questions that would soon be fired at him.

Jack turned toward Annie and furrowed his brows. Annie pursed her lips and shrugged her shoulders. It was no use. He would tell them everything they wanted to know. She sighed.

"I'm part owner of Powells Transportation Service. We have four vans, two limos, and we also rent out bicycles, mopeds, and Segways for those who like to tour the city by themselves. We also have a vacation rental business. My sister handles that."

Annie drew in a deep taste of her tea as she awaited the sighs from her grandmother and auntie. She held the cup to her mouth, and when she didn't hear any sounds of disapproval, she removed the cup. "Isn't that wonderful? His family has been in business for years." Annie nodded while grinning.

"Yes, it is. What is it you do for the company?" Lilly asked.

Annie glanced at her watch. "Oh, gosh, Jack, we

have to run. Our movie is starting soon. We don't want to be late." Annie removed Jack's cup from his hand and set it down on the table. She reached over and grabbed his hand, pulling him up from the sofa. The puzzled look on his face told her he was confused, but he went along with the charade.

"Thank you for the tea. It was so nice meeting you," Jack said as Annie pulled him along toward the front door.

"I'll talk to you soon." Annie rushed toward the front door and pulled it open. She practically shoved poor Jack out onto the front stoop. She gave a haphazard wave to the old ladies and then pulled the door shut.

"That was a close call." Annie took in a sharp intake of breath. She could feel the warming of her face and neck, and wondered how red she was getting.

"What was that all about?" Jack asked as he opened the car door for Annie.

Annie relaxed her shoulders, slumping over just a bit. The corners of her mouth turned down as she lowered her head. "It's a long story."

Jack reached out and lifted her chin. "How about a cup of coffee and a cupcake?" His eyes twinkled.

CHAPTER 6

"First of all, thank you for your dad's service to this country. If he were here, I'd shake his hand. This town is full of military heritage."

"Yes, he graduated with honors from The Citadel. He always said he was born to serve." Annie blinked back the tears trying to roll down her cheek.

"Your family must be very proud. You mentioned he died in a car accident."

"Yes. He had two tours in Afghanistan and came home unscathed, only to be killed by a drunk driver." Annie lowered her gaze to the cupcake, picked it up, and peeled back the paper liner.

"That's terrible," he whispered.

"I feel bad for my grandmother. It's not right to bury your children."

"Indeed."

She crossed her legs at the ankles, one foot juddering rapidly as she eyed the cupcake. Finally, she brought the chocolate delight to her mouth.

Jack leaned back in his chair and studied her face. She quickly grabbed a napkin. "What? Do I have crumbs all over my face?"

He laughed. "No, I was just thinking about Lilly and Patty. I know they only want the best for you. If I had a daughter or a granddaughter even, I'd want the same. But I can't help but think there is something you're not telling me," he said, peering at her through half closed lids.

She drew in a taste of her coffee, wiping the dribble that escaped her mouth with the nearby napkin. "My family is quite wealthy, but you wouldn't know it because I rather live a more simple life. But, Mary and I are going to inherit quite a bit someday. Hopefully, a long time from now, but in the interim, my father had set up a trust account, and it's coming due soon. They're just concerned that someone might use me for my money."

"Ah, I see." He took a bite of his chocolate salted

caramel cupcake. "This flavor is so satisfying. It's like sweet and salty all in one." He smiled.

"I'm going to be a spinster my entire life." Annie slumped back in her chair.

Jack laughed. "No, you won't. But, you might have to be firmer with your grandmother and auntie. I tell you what. Would they enjoy a boat ride out to the island? We could do another picnic. They could get to know me and see that I'm not that bad after all. In fact, that little piece of land we own is worth quite a bit, not to mention the family business." He reached out and patted her hand.

"It should never be about someone's financial worth. It should be more about how they treat their fellow man, what's in their heart," Annie said, lowering her tone.

"Old people can be set in their ways, judgmental. But, it's up to our generation to show them the errors of their ways." Jack laced his fingers with hers.

He had a point. It was time to break the mold and throw off the shackles of prejudice in every form. "Okay, let's do it. What day?" Annie said with a hint of gleam in her eyes.

*C*onvincing her grandmother and auntie would prove to be a little more challenging than she'd first thought, but the rebel in her wouldn't let her give up. Some things were worth fighting for, and Jack was one of them.

"Please, Grandmother Lilly. It will be so much fun. Jack is a great driver, and his boat is very comfortable. It would mean so much to me."

"I don't know. I haven't been on a boat in ages." Lilly turned to Patty. "Any objections?"

"No, I'm keen on the idea." Patty smiled.

"Thank you, Auntie Patty." Annie gave her a big hug.

"What about me?"

Annie pursed her lips and cocked her head to the left. She took the few steps over to Grandmother Lilly's chair, wrapped her arms around her shoulders, and squeezed her. "I love you, Grandmother Lilly. In all of your grumpiness, too."

Grandmother Lilly made a humph noise.

Annie laughed. "Okay, so we're all set. We'll come by Sunday at around ten o'clock. We'll have you back in time for your two o'clock nap … I mean tea time." Annie's eyes twinkled.

CHAPTER 7

*A*fter a long day at Sweet Indulgence, Annie and Buffy headed home. It was a beautiful afternoon with just a hint of coolness in the air. Suddenly Annie's stride came to a halt. She looked over her shoulder only to find Buffy rolling in something.

Annie tugged on her leash. "Buffy, what are you doing?" She leaned over and peered at the area getting a whiff of an awful foul smell. "Oh, Buffy! Now you're going to need a bath."

A car slowly passed them, stopping suddenly. A man dropped the window down and peered out.

"Jack!"

"Hi. Need a lift?" He smiled.

"I'm almost home, silly. Besides, you wouldn't want

Ms. Stinky in your car. She found something disgusting and rolled in it."

Jack pulled his head back and laughed. "I can help."

A car honked at Jack. He pulled in his head and then pulled the car over to the curb. The other car quickly raced by, spraying her with water from the recent rain. She glared at the car as it sped past.

"Now two of us will need baths," Annie said disgustedly.

"Hop in. I don't care if you're stinky," Jack said.

"Not me — Buffy."

"I know, silly. Get in."

Annie climbed in the passenger seat after settling Buffy into the back seat.

"Wow, she's ripe. What the heck did she roll in?" Jack asked as he turned on the air conditioner full blast and recycled the air.

"It looked like rotten fruit, or …"

"Don't say it. Let's just stick with fruit as the answer," Jack said.

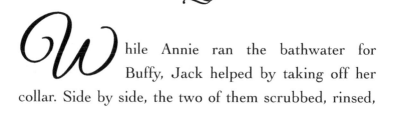

hile Annie ran the bathwater for Buffy, Jack helped by taking off her collar. Side by side, the two of them scrubbed, rinsed, and repeated as Buffy stood looking like a drowned rat.

"Oh, she's cold. She's shivering," Jack said, wrapping her in a fluffy towel.

"Bring her in the bedroom. I'll use the blow dryer on her."

Jack held Buffy while Annie blew dry her coat. "Does she like to be brushed?" Jack asked.

"She tolerates it," Annie said.

"This calls for a glass of wine," Jack said, looking down at his grimy and wet clothes.

Annie poured two glasses of merlot. Motioning to her couch, she invited him to sit. "I'm sorry you got so dirty."

"No worries. I'm glad to help. I hope she enjoys being clean," he said.

"I'm glad we ran into each other," Annie said, smiling.

"Well, I stopped by the bakery first and you'd already closed. I figured you were on your way home."

"Ah, so you planned it," Annie said as she leaned into him, hitting his shoulder.

"How about I take you out for a bite to eat?" Jack asked, taking a sip of his wine.

"Nah, let's stay in. Do you like ramen? I lived on that stuff while I was in college and I still like it," Annie said, getting up from the couch and crossing over to the kitchen.

Ramen made everything better, especially on a cool evening such as this. After they finished dinner, she poured their second glass of merlot, dimmed all the lights, and switched on the television. With Buffy curled up in her bed, exhausted from chewing her bone after her bath, Annie and Jack cuddled on the sofa, proud of their accomplishments.

They were laughing at the show, *Funniest Home Videos*, when her phone began to dance all over the glass coffee table. She quickly reached for the vibrating phone.

"We'd like to have you over for supper. Some financial papers came that we need to discuss."

"What kind of paperwork?" Annie covered the phone and mouthed, "Grandmother" to Jack.

Jack raised his finger to his mouth, showing her he'd be closemouthed during the conversation.

"I have a very busy schedule. I'm trying to coordinate something with Vicky and the girls and Jack."

"Jack Powell?"

"Yes." Annie dared her to say anything about it.

"When can we expect you?" Grandmother Lilly said, not missing a beat.

Annie sighed into the receiver. "I'll stop by tomorrow."

"Everything okay?" Jack asked.

"Yes. I have to read over some paperwork that came in regarding my inheritance."

"Oh." Jack set his glass down. "Maybe I should be going, then."

"No, you don't need to go. Please stay."

Jack nodded. "Alright."

They continued to laugh at the crazy stunts on the show and soon Annie couldn't even remember the conversation she'd had with her grandmother. After the show, Annie walked Jack to the door. "Thanks again for helping me. Giving her a bath can be such an ordeal."

"You're welcome. And thanks for dinner ... and the wine." He winked.

"Ramen and merlot, the dinner of champions."

Jack reached out and gently stroked her arm. "I had a great time tonight. It was just the sort of evening I like to spend."

"Eating ramen and drinking wine?"

"That, and ..." He pulled her into his arms. "And this." His mouth met hers in a soft kiss. She dropped her arms by her side. His sweet warm breath lingered just above her lips. He stepped back, brushing his hand through his hair.

"Hey, you can come back anytime to help me give Buffy a bath," she said with a twinkle in her eyes.

"As long as you serve me ramen and merlot." He gave her a quick peck and then he was gone.

～

*A*nnie tossed the document back onto the table. "If I'm reading this correctly, it looks like I'm inheriting the last of the money. What about Mary?"

"Well, she is to get her share on her twenty-sixth birthday as well, but they've provided for her handsomely as they did you in the interim."

Annie nodded.

"And of course, the house is in both of your names after we're both gone," Grandmother Lilly said.

"I don't want to talk about that right now. You're not going anywhere." Annie rapped her fingers on the table.

"What are you going to do with that large amount of money?" Auntie Patty asked.

"I don't really know. I'll see a financial advisor and discuss the possibilities. I've always wanted to own a house."

"But you'll get this house when we're gone," Grandmother Lilly blurted out. "It must stay in the family forever."

"We won't sell it, I promise. Maybe Mary will enjoy living here. I think I'll take some of the money and expand my business. Open a second cupcakery perhaps."

"Child, you have a lot of ambition, and that's great, but we'd like to see you settle down, too," Grandmother Lilly said.

Annie slapped her hands to her hips. "I don't need a man in my life to make me successful, or whole, or however you two old ladies think I should feel. I want to live my life the way I want to, and you need to stop meddling." Annie was surprised by her temper and softened her face. "I'm sorry. I didn't mean to yell."

"Or call us old ladies?" Auntie Patty said, turning her back on Annie.

"I apologize for the outburst. I don't mean any disrespect," Annie said, feeling badly about her eruption.

"Not many young women at the age of twenty-six have as much going for them as you do. You will be worth a lot of money, and soon. This Jack Powell fellow may not be worthy of you." Grandmother Lilly lifted her chin and shrugged her shoulders, turning away from Annie before she could answer her face-to-face.

"Grandmother … that's not fair. You have refused to even get to know him. He wanted to take you on a boat ride, get to know you guys. Please." A tear rolled down Annie's cheek.

"Okay, we'll go on the boat ride, but nothing more," Grandmother Lilly spewed.

CHAPTER 8

"*A*re you nervous?" Jack asked Annie on the drive over to pick up her grandmother and auntie.

"No. Well, yes, a little," she squeaked out.

"It's going to be all right. I can handle myself, and I can certainly handle two seventy-something-year-olds." He winked.

Annie heaved her shoulders up and down and let out a long sigh. "I sure hope so. You won't be the first guy they've chased away." She poked out her bottom lip.

"*A*untie Patty, grab your sunhat," Annie said, pointing to the bright yellow hat sitting on the table.

"Jack, be a dear and fetch the picnic basket. It's in the kitchen," Grandmother Lilly said.

Annie shrugged her shoulders at Jack.

"This is pretty hefty. What's in here?" He moved the basket up and down in his hand.

"I made pimento cheese sandwiches, potato salad, and brownies," Grandmother Lilly said.

"Sounds delicious." He gave Annie another wink.

Annie blushed. "Okay, let's go."

The drive out to the dock was fairly quiet. Every now and then, one of the older ladies would point out something along the way, and either Jack or Annie would comment. Once they arrived, Jack quickly opened the driver's side back door and helped out Auntie Patty. Annie watched him as he gently helped her out as she extended her own hand to Grandmother Lilly. Auntie Patty quickly laced her arm with Jack's while he juggled the picnic basket in the other.

One by one, Jack and Annie helped get the old women in the boat and settled. Each time the boat bounced or hit a wave, the women shrieked. Annie smiled when she witnessed Auntie Patty wiping the mist from the light spray that shot overboard off her grandmother's cheeks.

"Look, they're smiling." Annie squeezed Jack's arm.

"Something about being in the fresh air and open water does that to people."

"Even crotchety old women?" Annie smiled.

"Even them." He playfully knocked shoulders with Annie.

Jack jumped off the boat and quickly tied her to the wooden dock. He helped Annie out first, and then one by one, they helped the old women out.

"Now, be careful, there is a bit of a hill," Jack cautioned as he guided Grandmother Lilly.

Annie loved Jack's patience with her grandmother and auntie. They could be such a pain in the butt. Once they got to the old and worn picnic table, both of the older women were breathing hard.

"Take a moment and catch your breath," Annie said.

"I think that's the most I've hiked in a long time," Auntie Patty said with a raspy voice.

"Grandmother Lilly, are you all right?" Annie sat down between them as she watched them with concern.

"Yes, dear. Just enjoying the beautiful view." She patted Annie's leg. "How'd you find this place?" Grandmother Lilly asked Jack.

"This has been in my family for a very long time. I come here often." He smiled toward Annie.

Grandmother Lilly glanced back and forth between the two, watching them flirt silently. "I see. Well, is anyone hungry?"

After a filling lunch, Jack and Annie left them and walked around. Once out of their view, she laced her arm in his. They walked silently, enjoying the sounds of nature when the sound of a snapping twig startled them. Jack caught Annie as she stumbled slightly, causing her to giggle.

Jack reached up and pushed her hair back and studied her face. He raised his fingers and caressed her cheek before gently guiding them down her mouth. Her stomach tightened in anticipation of what came next.

She rolled her bottom lip between her teeth and waited for more. He tilted her chin and laid a soft, wet kiss on her lips, his tongue dipping in between the seams of her mouth. Annie leaned in harder, deeper, and wrapped her arms around his neck, holding him there. They kissed for a few moments when they heard the sounds of rustling leaves.

"Grandmother!" Annie shouted.

Annie rushed toward her grandmother. "You shouldn't have walked here by yourself. You could have fallen, or worse." Annie looked back at Jack and winced.

"We're getting tired. It was a lovely day, but we're worn out."

"Okay, let's get these adventurous women back to their house." Jack took one of Lilly's arms, and Annie had the other.

~

*H*e pulled up in front of the cigar shop and cut the engine. He turned toward Annie, putting his arm on the steering wheel. "I think they had a great time."

"Oh, yes, they sure did. I think they'll sleep just fine tonight." She locked her eyes onto his.

"When I spend a day outdoors, I sleep like a baby," Jack said.

"That and the glass or two of wine or scotch will have them snoring." Annie laughed at the vision of her grandmother and auntie sleeping with eye covers on and snoring.

"I think they liked me." Jack nodded.

Annie smiled. "I think so. I'll hear more about it during my next Sunday dinner."

"I'm already thinking of things I can do to win them over. Do you think they'd enjoy meeting my family?"

Annie twirled her finger around the ends of her hair and gave a little shrug. "I know I'd like to meet them."

Jack slapped the steering wheel. "Why, of course. I'll set something up, but I have to warn you. My family is crazy."

Jack opened the car door and jogged to the passenger side, helping Annie out. He walked her to the door, and they stood holding hands.

"I really had a good time today. I'm not just saying that either. My family is very important to me, and I know yours is to you as well." He pulled her toward him.

She heaved her shoulders when she drew in a long breath. "Yes, my loving, but very bossy family. They're all I have."

Jack ran his thumb in circles over hers. He leaned in and laid another warm kiss on her lips.

CHAPTER 9

*A*nnie changed her clothes exactly four times. She stared at her reflection in the long mirror that hung from the back of her bedroom door. She shook her head rapidly. "None of this is appropriate." She tore off the scarf wrapped around her neck and began to undress. The phone rang in the other room, breaking her concentration.

"Are you sure you don't want me to come and get you, and then we go pick them up?"

"No, I got it. I think it's better if I drive."

"Faster escape?" Jack asked.

Annie laughed into the phone. "You've met my grandmother and auntie I see."

"Listen, they'll be fine. I can't wait for you to meet my family."

Annie hung up the phone, and then with her hands on her hips, eyed her wardrobe for the umpteenth time.

"*A*untie Patty, Grandmother Lilly," Annie blurted. "You're so … so … dressed up." Annie pulled her brows together forming a V.

"We always dress up when we are invited to someone's home for dinner," Grandmother Lilly stated.

"Yes, but this is not a formal dinner. This is casual, a barbeque." Annie huffed.

Grandmother Lilly squared her shoulders. Auntie Patty made a humph noise and then breathed in deeply, sighing as she let the air out of her lungs.

"Oh, come on. We don't have time to change." Annie herded them toward the front door.

Grandmother Lilly twisted her head slightly. "Change? Who said anything about changing?"

Annie placed her hands on her grandmother's and auntie's shoulders. "Walk," she ordered.

*A*nnie wiped her sweaty palms down the legs of the white capris she'd decided to wear. She straightened her back and then rapped on the door. In a matter of moments, the front door flew open and there stood Jack. Annie's eyes darted around the room behind him. Bobbing heads and the clatter of laughter filled the space.

"Please, come in." Jack took Annie's hand. He gave each older woman a peck on the cheek. When they all got inside the house, Jack made the introductions. "Mom, this is Annie."

"It's so nice to meet you," she said, holding onto her hand. "Please call me Milly."

Annie enjoyed the warmness of Jack's mom's hand. "This is my grandmother Lilly and auntie Patty." Annie motioned toward the old women.

Jack's mom embraced each member of Annie's family. "Welcome to our home. Please, come in and have a seat."

Jack held Annie back as his mother took her grandmother and auntie to the living room. "See? I told you everything would be all right. My family is going to adore them, and they are going to completely fall in love with you." He pulled her close for a hug.

Jack pulled Annie along and announced her to the

gang that was waiting in the living room. "Everyone, this is Annie," Jack shouted.

A low and loud voice yelled hello from one corner. From another, a high voice shouted a hello. Every corner, every inch of that room had a body, and from that body called out a greeting to Annie. She smiled, repeated the hellos, and soon she was the center of attention.

A slender dark-haired woman approached her, holding hands with a little girl.

"You must be Diane. And you," Annie said, stooping over and meeting the gaze of the young child, "must be Crystal."

"This is my husband, Richard," Diane said. "We've heard so much about you." Diane pulled up the corners of her mouth in a warm smile.

"I've heard a lot about you as well."

"You guys can talk later. I want Annie to meet the grandparents." Jack took Annie by the hand and led her to another area of the room.

Annie's eyes bobbled back and forth from her grandmother and auntie to the other older folks sitting nearby. She strained her ears some to listen. Her stomach clenched tightly in anticipation of what she might hear.

"Dear, these are Jack's grandparents," Grandmother Lilly blurted when she caught sight of Annie.

Annie shook hands with Jack's grandparents on both sides, Polly, Bert, Russell, and Cora. She wondered if she'd ever get all the names straight. She committed them to the database in her brain and felt somewhat confident on recalling them later, until she heard the word cousins. She relaxed her shoulders, and tired from smiling so much, relaxed her smile, too.

"Come on, I think you need some air." Jack led her outdoors. "Stop worrying about them. How much trouble could some seventy-year-old women be?" Jack smiled.

Annie laughed. "I need a drink, and make it a double."

CHAPTER 10

*A*nnie waited in the baggage area for Mary. She glanced at her watch as she paced. Morgan was holding down the fort at the bakery, and Annie felt comfortable leaving it in her more than capable hands. But, she being the control freak that she was, she felt it necessary to be there at all times.

"Annie!"

Annie twirled around to find her sister bouncing toward her. "Mary." Annie embraced her in a warm hug. "How was the flight?"

"Good. Long, but good. I'm so glad to be home." Mary's eyes twinkled.

"I see you got a bit of sun." Annie touched Mary's arm, admiring her golden tan and wishing she'd inherited their mother's bronze complexion like Mary had.

"You must go to Europe. It's so beautiful. I think my favorite country was Italy." Mary looked back toward the luggage carousel. "I see my bag," she said and took off to retrieve it.

"Grandmother and Auntie are going to be so happy to see you. They've been worried about you."

"I'll be booked for Sunday dinners for the next several weeks. They won't let me off the hook, will they?" Mary laughed.

"Well, if they won't let me off they surely will not let you off." Annie laced her arm with Mary's. "Let's go home."

Mary tossed her large duffle bag in Annie's trunk and then took her place in the passenger seat up front. They chatted about all the places she'd visited and she promised to show Annie pictures, too.

"So, what have you been up to? Still working hard at the bakery?"

"Yes, the bakery is doing great. In fact, I just expanded Morgan's hours." Annie kept her eyes on the road as she spoke.

"That's great. Maybe I can pick up some hours now that I'm back."

Annie glanced at Mary. "Oh? I didn't think you'd want to. I mean, don't you want to start looking for employment?"

"Working at your bakery is employment," Mary said.

"Yes, but a real job. Well, you know what I mean. Something in the area of your degree, perhaps?" Annie thought about all the money they'd shelled out for her education.

"I don't know what I want to do," Mary said as she looked out the window.

Annie glanced over at her and stared at the back of Mary's head before turning her eyes back to the road.

*A*nnie pulled over on the curbside in front of the house.

"Aren't you coming in?" Mary asked.

"I have to get back to the bakery. Besides, you have a lot of catching up to do with them." Annie nodded toward the large stucco house one row back from the waterway.

Mary raised her brow. "Uh huh, sure ... okay, I get it, but you know you'll have to rescue me at some point." Mary got out of the car. Annie rolled down the window as she popped the lid to the trunk. Mary leaned in. "I'm going to move out."

"Move out! Move where? You can't just drop that on them your first day home."

"I know, but I am going to move."

"Don't you need a job first?"

"I do. I'm going to work at the bakery with you." Mary stepped back and smiled.

Annie watched her from the rearview mirror as she got her bag out of the trunk. Her eyes traveled with Mary as she made her way to the front of the house. *Work with me?* She slumped in the car seat.

~

*M*organ looked up as Annie entered the shop. Annie eyed the display case and did a quick inventory. "Looks like you made some sales," Annie said.

"We've been super busy. I haven't had a minute to catch my breath."

The door opened causing them both to look.

"See what I mean?" Morgan looked at Annie and then smiled at the customer. "How can I help you?"

"I'd like a dozen cupcakes, a variety," the older gentleman said.

Annie watched as Morgan served the man. She no

sooner got him taken care of, and the door opened again. This time a young woman entered.

"I'd like a dozen cupcakes, please," she said.

Annie rapped her fingers on the glass top of the display unit. Her business was doing well. She didn't have any complaints, but this seemed odd that all of these folks were coming in buying dozens of cupcakes.

"Excuse me, miss," Annie said.

The young woman smiled.

"I don't believe I've seen you in here before. Is this your first visit?"

"Yes, I didn't even know it was here. I'm renting a house out on one of the islands, and the limo driver who picked me up from the airport told me about your place."

Annie gulped. *Jack.* "Do you remember the guy's name?"

"Yes, I have his card." The woman dug in her purse.

Annie held the corners of the card as she read the words. *Powell Limousine Services.*

It went on like that for the next hour. Annie and Morgan served up customer after customer until the display case was empty and they had to turn the closed sign on the front door. Annie stood with her back up against the door. "That was insane."

"What was insane?" Morgan asked.

"What just happened here today. Don't you see? Just by word of mouth, my business went from selling a couple of dozens a day to completely selling out in one afternoon. I have to thank him." Annie pushed off from the door and crossed over to where Morgan stood.

"Thank him? Thank who?" Morgan tilted her head as she waited for the answer.

"Jack Powell," Annie whispered.

CHAPTER 11

*S*he practically jogged home that afternoon, with her mind racing about what she'd say to Jack. She tossed her keys on the table and called for Buffy as she eyed the place for any puddles. She'd missed out on her walk because Annie had left her home that day. Buffy wagged her tail and danced around the table legs as Annie secured her leash.

Buffy sniffed all of her favorite bushes and stopped to do her business along the way. Annie held her phone tightly, every now and then looking at the screen. After a few minutes, Annie found a vacant bench and sat down. Buffy, now content, lay by her feet, breathing in the salt air, Annie laughed as she watched her sniffing away, catching scents here and there. She looked at her phone once again. She hit the button and waited.

"Hey, Jack."

"Hey, there. Did you get your sister picked up from the airport?"

"Yes, and I dropped her off at Grandmother's so she could visit and I came back to the bakery." Annie tried to lead him to confess.

"Ahh, that's good. I can't wait to meet her."

"Yes, but I have to warn you. She's nothing like me. She's a bit flighty."

"Well, she's young. Didn't you say she's twenty-two?"

"Yes, and she thinks she's going to come work for me and move out of Grandmother's house."

"You could use the extra help."

"How do you know I need the extra help?" Annie challenged him, hoping he'd confess now.

"Because you told me. You told me you'd recently given Morgan more hours."

"Oh, yes, I did do that. Well, something really strange happened today." Could the business card just be a coincidence, she wondered. "Morgan became swamped with customers while I was gone. When I returned, we had more. In one hour we sold out of cupcakes, and I had to put the closed sign up."

"That's great! Don't you want that kind of business?"

"I do, but I found it strange that it occurred so quickly." Annie recalled the business card once again. "Listen, a lady came in and she said you sent her." Annie felt it best to just come out with it.

Jack laughed into the phone. His laugh was deep and steady.

"What's so funny?" Annie asked.

"I wondered when you'd say something."

"Are you telling people about the cupcakery?"

"I am. Every chance I get."

"How nice of you, Jack. I mean it. It actually gave me a great idea. I need to branch out more and advertise."

"I'd be happy to help you. I'll take a bunch of flyers and business cards, and wherever I stop to pick up customers, I'll spread the word."

"You'd do that for me?"

"I would. I'd do that and more, if you'd let me."

Annie drew in a deep breath. Her heart began to beat rapidly and she could feel the warmth rush through her entire body, landing on her cheeks and turning them bright red. Annie swallowed down the large lump that formed in her throat. "I'd like to see you again. I'd like to thank you for your kindness—in person."

"I'd hardly be able to resist a personal thank you," Jack teased.

"Why don't you come over for dinner?"

"That would be great. Can I bring something?" Jack asked.

Just your big strong hands. "How about a bottle of wine?"

～

*T*he lasagna baked to a golden brown. The sourdough bread was sliced and warm. The salad was chopped and waiting to be drenched in a homemade dressing. Dessert was cupcakes, of course. Annie set the small table and lit the candles. "Now, you be on your best behavior." She playfully shook her finger at Buffy. Annie turned toward the door when she heard the light rap. "What are you doing here?"

"I couldn't take one more minute of them. I needed wine." Mary brushed past Annie and went straight to the fridge.

Annie slammed the door shut.

"What?" Mary said, poking her head out from the fridge.

"I have company coming that will be here any minute. You can't stay."

Mary's eyes glanced to the table. A wide smile swept across her face. "You're having a guy come to dinner!"

"Yes, and he'll be here any second. Please leave," Annie begged. She laced her arm in Mary's and pulled her toward the front door.

"Okay, but I want all the details tomorrow." Mary leaned in and kissed her sister's cheek.

Annie pulled open the front door. Both women gasped.

"I'm sorry, did I startle you?" Jack asked.

Mary smiled.

"This is my sister, Mary," Annie said, motioning with her hand.

Jack took Mary's hand and shook it. "Nice to meet you. You're just back from Europe I hear."

"Yes—"

"And, she'll tell us about it another time, right, Mary?" Annie ushered her out the door.

Mary twirled around, stretching her neck to find Jack. "Yes, I will look forward to telling you all about it."

Annie closed the door halfway, sticking her neck out between the door frame and door. "Good night, Sister."

Mary brushed her long golden locks back with her hands. "Sheesh, Annie. You don't have to be so rude. I get it when I'm not welcomed."

"It's not that," Annie called out.

Mary stopped and turned toward Annie. "He's gorgeous."

Annie dropped her gaze. She brought her head up and smiled. "Yeah, I know, now good night."

Annie shut the door and turned around. Jack dug his hands into his pockets and smiled.

"Hungry?" Annie asked as she brushed past him to get the dinner ready for serving.

"Starving."

In between bites, Jack took the opportunity to let her know how good the food tasted. He didn't really have to tell her, his third helping of lasagna told her that. Jack grabbed his stomach. "I'm going to explode. But everything was delicious."

"Thank you. Any room for dessert?"

"No way," Jack grumbled.

"How about we move to the couch and let our dinner digest? Then maybe we'll have room," Annie said, leading the way.

"What about the dishes?"

"Let them soak, I'll get to them later." She set her wine glass down on the coffee table and plopped down on the sofa. Jack followed suit.

"I wanted to let you know that I stopped by the

printing store and ordered five hundred flyers. I really appreciate you helping me."

"I'm happy to."

"Thanks for being a good sport about Mary, too. I told you she's a handful."

"No worries."

"I have to find something for her to do. I don't want her working with me. She'll drive me crazy."

"Your grandmother and auntie seemed to get along pretty good, and they're sisters."

"Oh, please. They have their moments. But Grandmother rules the household. Auntie Patty goes along with most of her shenanigans. But, they do love each other." Annie softened her expression.

"And you love Mary," Jack offered.

Annie nodded.

"Families. We don't get to choose them, and they make us angry and crazy sometimes, but at least they're ours, and no one can deny us that." Jack took a sip of his wine.

Annie put the wine glass to her mouth and drew in a taste. "True," she said, holding the glass in her hands.

"I'm always looking for extra help … maybe I could help?"

"No, this is a family matter. We'll work it out."

Jack scooted a little closer to her. "Hey, what about

that thing you said earlier on the phone." He nuzzled her neck, giving her a fluttering feeling in her tummy.

She leaned forward, putting her glass down again. She sat back and turned slightly toward him. They gazed into each other's eyes and then at the very same moment, leaned in for a kiss. Annie closed her eyes tightly as she savored his warm mouth. She clung to his broad shoulders as he deepened the kiss, his sweet warm breath with a hint of wine lingering on her lips. She followed his lead and teased him with her tongue.

After a few moments, he pulled back. "You can thank me anytime you want." He winked.

She blushed. "Jack, I really do owe you a debt of gratitude for helping me spread the word about Sweet Indulgence." She reached out and took his hands in hers.

"Nonsense. Your cupcakes are the best. People need to know about them. " He gave her a quick kiss on the mouth.

"Thank you for saying that."

"What about those dishes?" Jack said, breaking the mood.

Annie followed him with her eyes as he made his way to the kitchen. She sighed, and then picking up her wine glass, headed to the kitchen where the dirty dishes waited.

"Is there anything you don't like to do?" Annie asked as she dried and stacked the clean dishes.

"Not really. But then again, I haven't done everything." He winked, then dipped his hands back into the sudsy water.

"Is there any kind of food you don't like?" She wanted to know for future dinners.

"Brussel sprouts."

"Me, too!" she said.

Once all the dishes were washed, dried, and put away, Jack announced he thought he now had room for dessert.

Annie uncovered the dish and brought it to the table where he waited with a fork in hand.

She laughed. "You have a bottomless pit."

"I love to eat," he teased, eyeing the mini cheesecakes.

∾

*J*ack leaned in and gave Annie a good night kiss she'd remember for a long time. She followed him with her eyes as he moved down the hall toward the steps that would take him out of the building.

"Wait." She closed the door behind her.

Jack stopped and turned. She traveled toward him quickly, and he swept her into his arms. She smoothed over his strong protective arms, wrapping her arms around his neck. She leaned back, her heart stumbling before finding its rhythm once again.

"I don't know where this is going, if it's going anywhere, actually." She studied his face. "But I do like you, Jack Powell."

He pulled her closer, his lips brushing against hers. "I like you, too, Annie McPherson." He raised her hand to his mouth and kissed it.

"Good night, Jack."

Annie watched as he made his way to the stairs. He glanced back at her just before he took the first step. Her face lit up with happiness when she witnessed the broad smile that crossed his face. Thrilled with how the evening ended, she moved down the hall to her front door and slowly entered the apartment.

CHAPTER 12

"*O*kay, just hear me out, Mary." Annie paced the room with one hand on her hip as she held the phone. "You can't just move out without money. Grandmother and Auntie paid for your very generous graduation present to Europe, but you don't really expect them to fund your new place, too, do you?"

"It's just a loan," Mary said.

"Mary, don't be ridiculous. What's your hurry?" Annie said.

"I need my own space," she replied.

"Space for what? To crash in your bed at night after being out with your friends?" Annie said, now reeling with anger.

"You wouldn't understand. You have your own place."

"Okay, Mary, listen up. I'm twenty-six years old. I lived with Grandmother and Auntie Patty until I was twenty-five. You're twenty-two. I'd say you have a few more years. And besides, I opened up my business and earned my own money. You're asking them to finance your apartment. That's not fair."

"They have more than they need. And, I know our parents left us a boatload of cash."

"Mary! I can't believe you said that. Is something else going on? I've never known you to be this outspoken or uncaring, especially when it involved Grandmother and Auntie Patty."

"Sort of."

"Okay, wait. Don't say another word. This calls for drinks around a table with music playing in the background, and where we can let our hair down and talk."

"And be sisters," Mary whispered.

"Yes. I'll pick you up at eight." Annie hung up the phone before letting Mary answer. She tossed the phone on the table and stared at it. "What is going on with you?"

"*Y*ou look cute in that outfit," Annie said to Mary as she hopped into the car.

"I bought it in Paris," she said as if she were singing a song.

Annie raised a brow. "Any questions or concerns from the old ladies who live there?" she asked, pointing toward the house with her chin.

Mary laughed. "Just the usual kind. Where are you going, who are you going with, and what time will you be home?" Mary twisted her mouth to the side.

Annie pulled up to the nightclub. "I'll park the car. You go grab us a table."

The place was dark, and the smell of old alcohol permeated the air along with some flowery spray the owners used to cover up the old alcohol smell. Annie spotted Mary and crossed the room toward the table. She hung her purse on the back of the chair and sat down. Picking up the drink menu, she scanned the exotic drinks listed.

"I think I'll just have a vodka Collins," Annie said, putting down the menu.

Mary caught the eye of the wandering server and waved. "I'll have a margarita on the rocks with salt, and she'll have a vodka Collins. Thank you."

"Sure, no problem. I'll be back with those drinks in a minute." He walked off.

"He's cute," Mary said, leaning in toward Annie.

Annie nodded. "Okay, so do we want to start talking before the drinks come?" Annie asked.

"No, let's wait."

They listened to the music and chatter from other club goers, and just as the server had said, he brought the drinks back quickly.

"Can we run a tab, please?" Annie smiled.

The cute server smiled back. "Sure, anything for the pretty ladies." He winked, causing Annie to blush.

Annie pulled her chair closer to the table. She drew in a taste of her drink with the straw and sighed. "Ooh la la, that's a tasty drink. Now, tell me what is going on."

"I met a guy."

Annie slumped back in her chair. She lowered her chin and stared at her drink. She raised her head and focused on Mary's eyes. "I see. Where?"

"Italy."

"And he's coming here?"

Mary nodded.

"That's why you think you need your own place?"

Mary nodded.

"That's exactly why you don't need your own place,

Mary!" Annie said causing a few people to look over at them.

"I want some privacy."

"You have that with Grandmother and Auntie Patty. You don't need your own place."

Mary picked up her drink and began to lick the salted rim.

"Once you have a good job, a little more life experience and money, then you can get your own place, and I'll support you one hundred percent. Let the guy come over if he wants to. Let him get his own place. Of course, I don't want to know any details if he does, but I'm just saying, it's not up to you. Who does he think he is, asking you to do this, anyway?"

"He didn't ask me, but it's hard to resist him." The corners of Mary's mouth turned up in a half smile.

"Resist him you shall. I mean it, Mary. Don't do anything you'll regret."

"You aren't my mother, Annie."

"No, but I'm your big sister, and I know if Mom or Dad were here, they'd tell you the same thing. You aren't ready for your own place. Once you have a good job and some money, then we'll talk. Otherwise, get used to it—you, Grandmother, and Auntie will be roommates a bit longer."

Mary made a humph sound and then drew in a taste of her drink.

"I love you, little Sister, I do. This is tough love talking right here. I hope you would do the same for me if it were reversed."

"I guess." Mary kicked the pole that held the tabletop on. The metal sound resonated for a second.

Annie peered at Mary through half-closed lids. "Let's start tomorrow by looking for jobs you can apply for. That's the first step."

"Okay. Thank you for helping me. I guess I'm trying to grow up too fast."

"Well, you're not really growing up too fast." Annie dropped her shoulders. She felt awful for chastising Mary. "You just want to spread your wings. There's a difference. I'll help you, I promise." She winked at her sister. "So, this Italian guy is really going to come all the way to the U.S. to see you?"

"Who said he was Italian?" Mary winked and then whirled around.

CHAPTER 13

"Mary has some good news to share," Grandmother Lilly said.

Annie put her fork down and gave Mary her full attention.

Mary flashed a smile to the group and then made her announcement. "I got a job!"

Annie clapped. "Yay! Where at?"

"Powell Vacation Rentals."

Annie's smile quickly turned to a frown. "Powell Vacation Rentals?"

Mary nodded.

Annie turned her attention to her grandmother. "You knew about this and didn't tell me?"

"What's wrong with her working there? They offered her the job."

"I feel as if you went behind my back," Annie said.

"That's ridiculous. We did no such thing. Jack contacted Mary."

Annie locked eyes with Mary. "Is that true? He called you?"

"Well, he didn't actually call me. He came by."

"Here? He came by here?"

Mary nodded. "Listen, Annie. He's a great guy. Don't be upset with him. He's just trying to help. I'm really excited about working with Diane."

Annie pushed her chair back and folded her hands in her lap. "I see. Well, I only met her once, but she seemed like a lovely person," Annie said. "Please don't do anything to embarrass the family or me."

"And, since we're dropping bombs here today, we might as well tell her the rest," Auntie Patty said.

Annie slumped in the chair, sighing as she did. "There's more?"

"We purchased a car for Mary."

Annie gasped.

"She needed reliable transportation to get to her new job," Grandmother Lilly said.

"Next you'll tell me you bought her a house or rented her an apartment," Annie said, snapping.

"Now, dear, don't get overdramatic here. It's a car

for Pete's sake. A used one at that," Grandmother Lilly said.

Annie shook her head rapidly. "I give up. You guys win. I wish you the best, Mary, I really do. But, please don't think that now because you're working with the Powells that I'm going to continue to see Jack or that anything will come of our relationship. You're on your own," Annie said. She rose from her seat, picking up her plate with unfinished food. "There are no guarantees in life. Isn't that what you always said?" Annie said, smirking toward her grandmother and auntie. She moved to the kitchen before they could answer.

"She'll soften her stance. Just give her time," Auntie Patty said.

"What I can't figure out is why she is behaving like Jack doesn't mean anything to her. You should have seen how fast she tried to get rid of me the other night when he was coming over for dinner. You don't light candles for a friend," Mary said.

Grandmother Lilly glanced over to Patty. "I'd say our girl is smitten with Jack but doesn't quite know how to massage the relationship."

"Grandmother, let her do it on her own. She'd never forgive any of us if we meddle. She's upset with us as it is because of the job thing. I really thought she'd be happy for me."

"She *is* happy for you. I guess she thought we blind-sided her. She'll come around." Grandmother Lilly picked up her wine glass. "To a new job."

"And to a new car," Patty added.

"Cheers!" Mary said. Mary's smile quickly faded when she saw Annie standing in the threshold with her hands on her hips. "What?" Mary asked.

"Oh, so now I'm excluded from the family toasts?"

Mary pushed her chair back and ran across the room and hugged Annie. "You're not mad, are you?"

"Not at all." She said, squeezing her tightly.

"Come over here, Annie. Raise your glass to your sister's new beginnings," Auntie Patty said.

Annie pushed away from Mary's embrace and crossed over to her drink. "Here's to your success, Mary. I hope you learn a lot, live a lot more—and be safe while doing it," Annie said, crinkling up her face.

Laughter broke out around the table and then Annie moved in between her grandmother and Patty. She motioned for Mary to join them. "Grab your glass."

The women held up their glasses and began tapping each other. Cheering broke out, and then Mary announced, "Bottoms up!"

After they'd downed their wine, Annie turned toward Mary. "Help me clear these dishes."

Once they were together in the kitchen, Annie took

advantage of them being alone. "Listen, I really am happy for you. I want you to know that."

Mary nodded.

"It's just that I don't know where things are going with Jack, exactly."

"Annie, stop it. Stop it right now. You know you like him."

"I do, very much, but I haven't had the best track record when it comes to relationships and the length of them." She lowered her head.

"It's a two-way street when it comes to relationships. Those guys … well, they are to blame just as much as you for it not working out. I'd say even more."

"Thank you for saying that. I'm always asking myself what I could have done better."

Mary grabbed Annie by the shoulders. "Nothing. You couldn't have done a thing better. They were either immature, or … immature." The girls broke out in laughter.

"It's great to have you home," Annie said with just a hint of watery eyes.

"It's great to be home," Mary said, nodding as she raised her brows.

"When do you report to work?"

"Tomorrow!"

"Show me what you're going to wear." She grabbed

Mary by the hand and off they went to Mary's bedroom.

~

*A*nnie kicked off her shoes into the closet and then proceeded to take off her jewelry. A nice hot shower was in order. As the stream of water ran over her head and down her body, Annie thought about how she'd approach the subject with Jack. She towel dried her body, slipped on a nightgown, and then pulled down the covers to her bed, slipping in between the crisp sheets. She picked up her cell phone and stared at it. It began to vibrate in her hand! It was Jack.

"How'd Sunday night dinner go?"

"It went great. Lots of sharing," she replied.

"Was Mary there?"

"Yes."

"Did she have any news to share?"

"Yes."

"Annie? What's wrong?"

"Nothing." She wondered how long the one-word answers would go. "It was a great dinner, and yes, Mary had lots of good news. Seems she got a new car."

"Ahh. A new car is always fun. What kind?"

"I'm not sure. We really didn't get to discuss that

because we were celebrating so much over her other good news."

"Other good news?"

"Jack Powell, stop playing with me."

Jack laughed into the phone. "Who's playing with who?"

"I know she's going to be working with Diane," Annie said.

"You're not mad about that, are you?"

"I was at first, but I think the experience will be good for her, and if Diane can put up with my crazy sister, more power to her."

Jack laughed again. "I tried to hint around that I might have something for her but you cut me off, saying it was a family matter. I wasn't sure how to approach it. I stopped by the other day while you were at work and just asked a simple question. She loves to travel, so what better place to work at than a travel agency of sorts?"

"Travel agency?"

"Well, it's more vacation rentals, but you are essentially helping to plan someone's vacation."

Annie smiled. "True. Yes, she's perfect for the job."

"And listen, no pressure about us. If it doesn't work out between us, we'll remain friends. Just ask all of my former girlfriends. I'm always their friend afterward."

Annie bobbed her head side to side. "All your former girlfriends?"

Jack dug his hands deep into his pockets. A light hearted laugh escaped his mouth. "Yeah, all two of them. Now, when can I see you again?" "

His charming ways sucked her right in. I'm interviewing help tomorrow and the next day. How about dinner midweek?"

"I'd like to take you on a boat ride again. I have the perfect place for us to go."

"A boat ride?"

"Yes. To the best seafood restaurant that can be accessed by car or boat!"

"That sounds like fun, Jack. I can't wait. See you then."

~

*M*organ worked the counter while Annie interviewed the applicants. The first one was a tall, slender young man, nineteen years young, and in his second year of college.

"What do you know about baking, Peter Jamison?" Annie asked as she looked over his application.

"Nothing, but I'm a fast learner." He beamed with his answer.

"Do you have any cash handling experience?"

"No, but—"

"I know. You're a fast learner," Annie said, finishing his sentence for him. Annie turned the application face down and sat back in her chair. "Why don't you tell me why you think I should hire you? And don't say it's because you're a fast learner." She lowered her chin and pursed her lips.

"I need the job. College is expensive."

"Go on."

"My mother works two jobs just to help me and to cover her own living expenses."

Annie nodded. "You do realize this is just a part-time job? Probably no more than twenty hours a week."

"I have another job, so that's perfect."

"You have another job?" Annie said.

"Yes, I work for Jack Powell."

Annie tossed her head back and laughed. So this is how Jack wanted it to play out. He hired Mary, and now she would hire one of his own. "Are you related to Jack?"

The young man excitedly shook his head. "I clean out the cars, wash, and wax them." He puffed out his chest.

"Do you generally work the weekends for Jack?"

"Yes."

"I have a couple of more applicants still to see." Annie pushed back her chair and stood. "It was nice meeting you today." She extended her hand.

She watched as the lanky boy walked out of the shop.

"One down, two to go," she hollered to Morgan as she iced cupcakes in the back.

Morgan appeared at the counter, brushing crumbs off her apron. "He seemed like a sweet boy."

"Boy? He's nineteen."

"Boy." Morgan turned and headed back to icing cupcakes.

The bell over the door rang, and Annie looked up. In walked a petite black girl. She had a beautiful smile.

"Hello," Annie said. "You must be Rebecca?"

The girl nodded as she extended her hand. "Rebecca Hutton."

"Please, have a seat," Annie said, motioning toward the chair.

Rebecca sat down and clasped her hands in front of her.

"It says on your application that you have cooking experience. Where did you get your training from?"

"My grandmother and mother."

Annie nodded. "I see. Do they own a restaurant?"

Rebecca gaffed at the idea. "No, we do a lot of

baking for church activities, and also we have a foodie truck."

"A foodie truck! How awesome."

"We have the Cajun on Wheels truck," Rebecca said.

"I love that truck. I get the Cajun flavored fries and the shrimp. The shrimp is so good," Annie said.

The young woman nodded.

"What kinds of things have you baked before?"

"Cupcakes, regular cakes, cornbread, cookies, bread, and muffins."

"I see. You do have a lot of experience. Are you going to college?"

"Yes, I have one semester left."

"What's your degree in?"

"My major is in business with a minor in hospitality and tourism."

"I'm only guaranteeing twenty hours a week. Is that good for you?"

"As long as it's during the week, yes. I work the food truck on Saturdays, and on Sundays I have church."

Annie nodded. "I think we could work that out. Right now, all the applicants can't work the weekends. I guess if I can get help during the week at least, I'll have some time off. Right now, it's just

Morgan and me." Annie looked back toward the kitchen.

"When will you make a decision?" Rebecca asked.

"I just did. You're hired."

Annie promised to call her later. She watched as Rebecca glided out the front door, clearly on cloud nine. Annie sat back and waited for the final applicant of the day. She glanced at her watch. She had about fifteen minutes and decided to make a mad dash to the little girl's room. "Hold down the fort," she called out to Morgan.

When she emerged from the bathroom, an older woman sat in the chair the applicants had all shared. "Can I help you?"

Morgan appeared quickly from the back and interrupted her. "She's here about the job."

"Oh, thanks, Morgan." Annie took a seat across from the older woman.

"I have a lot of experience. I hope you won't discount me because of my age."

Thinking fast, she began with a refusal of any such thing. "Of course not. We don't care about age here." She laughed.

"Good. I have twenty-five years of baking experience. I used to make wedding cakes for a living."

"Oh, well, that's good to know. Why did you stop?"

"I still make them for friends and family, but I closed the shop doors a few years back. It was just too much keeping the place up, paying all the bills, and hiring people. I can sympathize with you on that." She nodded.

"Are you available on weekends?" Annie cut right to the chase.

"I could be. I'm retired, so one day is like the next for me. Every day is the weekend." She smiled.

"You're hired."

"Don't you want to know my name?"

Annie laughed. She picked up the woman's application and scanned it. "You're hired, Mrs. Walker."

"Please, call me Betsy."

"Betsy. And, I'm very pleased to meet you. I think we'll work just fine together."

CHAPTER 14

*V*ery few words were spoken between them. She enjoyed the quietness they shared. The way he guided her with his hand gently placed on her back, the way he softly pushed the stray strands of hair out of her eyes, or when he laced his fingers with hers. These were unspoken words. Words she bathed in and reciprocated by circling his thumb with hers, reaching up and cupping his hand as he swept the tendrils away, or how the hair on the back of her neck stood up and she quivered when he placed his hand on the small of her back.

"Here we are," Jack said as he pulled back the throttle and eased the boat into a berth. He jumped out of the boat and tied her up and then extended his hand to Annie.

"I've never been here before. I've wanted to come, though," Annie said as she glanced around.

"Wait until you taste their oysters." He ushered her down the dock toward the restaurant.

Oysters. Hmm. Did he really think she'd fall for the old aphrodisiac trick? "Oysters? I'm not a fan of them, sorry."

"Really? You don't say. No problem. They have many great items on their menu."

They waited for the host to seat them. Annie glanced around the dining area. "I hope I've dressed all right," she said, looking down at her black slacks and flat black shoes.

He tilted her chin up with his finger. "You look beautiful," he said, resting his hand on the shoulder of her purple satin blouse.

The host led the way to a table for two near the window that looked out to the inlet. Annie sighed. "It's a gorgeous night."

The host pulled back her chair. "Yes, it is," he said. "Your server will be here shortly."

"This place has such ambiance. I'm so happy you brought me here tonight," Annie said, smiling.

Jack leaned in.

"Good evening," a waiter holding menus said.

Jack pulled back and sat deep in his chair. The

server began with the specials of the evening. Jack held up a hand to stop him when he heard oysters. "I just told her how delicious they are here, but she's not a fan. What other specials do you have tonight?" Jack said, looking at the server.

He rattled off the remaining specials then turned to Annie.

"For the Ms.?"

"I'll have the flounder, please."

"Sir?"

"Oysters, please. Oh, and may we see the wine list?" Jack requested.

The server nodded. "Any appetizers to start?"

Annie shook her head.

"House salad or Caesar?"

"House for me with ranch," Jack said.

"I'll have the same," Annie said, thinking how lovely things were going.

Jack reached across the table and Annie placed her hands in his. "Annie, there's been something I've wanted to tell you."

Ah ha. Was he going to come clean about sending the kid about the job at the bakery?

"I know we just met, but something about you makes me feel like we've known each other for a long time."

"I feel like that as well. From the first day you walked into Sweet Indulgence, I was drawn to you. I guess it could be fate that you came in that day looking for cupcakes for Crystal."

"Yeah, I didn't tell you the entire story. See, I was asked to order those cupcakes from the grocery store bakery and I forgot. Diane had a million things going on, so I volunteered to take something off her plate. I panicked that morning when I realized that I had failed to do the one job she assigned me. I did a Google search, and your cupcakery popped up. I prayed so hard that you'd be open, and that you'd have two dozen cupcakes." He squeezed her hand.

"It was your lucky day in more ways than one." She squeezed his hand back.

Jack tilted his head, and when he did, the lights in the restaurant and the lights outside reflecting on the water added sparkle to his eyes. Annie focused on them hard.

Jack slowly released her hand, sitting back in his chair. He took his hand and brushed it through his dark wavy hair and then placed his hands on his lap. "You got that right, Annie. You saved me from being the awful uncle, and you kept me from living the life of a monk." He laughed.

"You, a monk? I hardly think that is possible." She lightly licked her dry lips.

He pushed a fork around and played with his water glass. "I was ready to give up on women."

Annie lifted her brow.

"Not give up on women as for good …"

Annie laughed. "I know what you mean. I almost gave up on men." She smiled.

"So can we mend these broken hearts of ours?" Jack asked.

Annie paused a moment, taking a long drink of her wine and savoring the taste of black cherry fruit, mineral, and tannin overtones. "I think with a little luck and a lot of practice, we can mend them."

Jack rubbed his jawline. "I'd like to try."

Annie leaned in across the table. He met her halfway. She began to lift herself up on her elbows to close the gap, but just then the server returned. She pulled back and sat down. The kiss would have to wait. It was just as well. Time would be the only test this relationship had to make it work. Like the great wine she just appreciated, nothing so beautiful could be created overnight. Especially over fish.

"Why didn't you tell me you were sending someone over to apply for the job at the bakery?"

"Busted." He laughed. "Well, did he make the cut?"

"He's a great kid, but he doesn't have a lick of experience in a store or bakery setting. Every time I asked him a question he followed it by—"

"I'm a fast learner?" Jack supplied.

"Yes, that."

"I know. He's young and doesn't have a lot of experience. But I have to tell you, he cleans my cars until they shine, and he's a hard worker. Just give him a chance, won't you?"

Annie lowered her gaze to the shining utensils on the table. Jack had a valid point. "I'll give him a chance. But I had two other applicants that are going to be so good for the bakery, that well, he's going to be the odd man out. Literally."

"Annie McPherson, are you gender biased?"

Annie raised her brows. "Of course not. If he could bake or do something I wouldn't even blink an eye."

"I know! He can be your janitor. I'm telling you, your shop will be the cleanest this side of Charleston."

Annie smiled from ear to ear. "Jack! That's a perfect solution. Thank you."

"I should be thanking you."

"Let's make a deal. If either Mary or …"

"Peter," Jack said.

"Peter—if either of them don't work out, we'll have to buy the other dinner."

Jack lifted his arm and put out his hand across the table. Annie took his hand and gave it a firm shake.

~

They were about fifteen minutes from the dock where Jack kept *Lady Powell* when it began to rain. Light rain fell at first, and then it seemed to drop in buckets. They huddled under the canopy of the boat, but the wind drove the rain inside, and it felt like bullets hitting their skin. The sky cracked, and bolts of lightning followed.

"It's getting wicked out here," Annie said.

"We'll be home soon," Jack said as the boat crested another wave. "I didn't expect the storm to hit now. The weatherman said it would hit around midnight."

Annie hit the button on the side of her watch, making the crystal face light up. "It's eleven thirty."

Jack tossed his head back and a deep throaty laugh escaped his mouth. "Time flies when you're having fun. No wonder they were giving us dirty looks. I think the restaurant closes at ten."

Another bolt of lightning startled Annie, drawing her closer to Jack. She laced her arms in his as he steered the boat. She sunk her face in his strong arm and closed her eyes.

"Now, you aren't afraid of a little summer storm, are you?" Jack said teasingly.

"A little." She poked her head out from the safety of his body.

"Look." He pointed in the distance. "Those are the lights from the dock."

"Oh, I can see them," Annie said, relieved.

Jack tied up the boat in record time, and the two ran as fast as they could to his car. She pulled down the visor that had a mirror and stared at the girl with mascara running down her face, her hair slicked against her skull, and cheeks rosy red, and laughed. She turned toward Jack and laughed some more.

"What? Do I have mascara running down my face, too?" He gently poked at her arm.

"No, silly. I was just thinking about how funny we must have looked running to the car."

Jack leaned across the seats and pulled her close. She gazed into his deep brown eyes, getting totally lost in them. He pulled her closer and their mouths touched. She wrapped her arms around his neck and held tightly, not wanting the kiss to stop. He must have got the message because he didn't stop kissing her until she relaxed her grip.

He sat back deep into the seat and stared out the windshield.

"What's wrong, Jack?"

"Nothing. Absolutely nothing. I need to get you home so you can dry off." He started the engine and turned on the wipers.

And the evening ended much like it began, with few words spoken and only the sounds of the wipers as it drew water across the windshield.

CHAPTER 15

*I*t was the first day of training at the bakery and Annie had it all planned that it would be a fun day as well as informative. Peter, Rebecca, and Betsy all arrived on time. That in and of itself brought a smile to Annie's face. She passed out the aprons and hair nets, and the five of them stood around the large stainless steel table that served as an island and went over the basics of making the batter.

"Any questions on what we went over here today?" Annie said.

Betsy raised her hand.

"Yes, Betsy?" Annie said.

"Are we all going to be bakers?"

"Good question. I would like everyone to learn all the different areas of the shop. Some of you will be better at baking, and some of you will be better with customer service." Annie smiled at Rebecca.

"What about me?" Peter said.

Nodding her head, Annie started off slow with her answer. "You'll learn these areas too, but because you have experience with cleaning, and I might add that Mr. Powell gave you a stellar recommendation, I thought you could help me best by keeping the shop clean." She locked eyes with him.

"That's cool. I can do that for you."

"Okay, great. Then it's settled. Icing the cupcakes takes a bit of more experience, and I think we'll leave that for another time. But by learning how to mix the batter and bake them, you'll be helping us tremendously. Tomorrow we'll go over the basics of the cash register. By next week, all of you will be on the schedule. If no one has any more questions, you're dismissed."

Annie turned and moved away from the group when she heard her name. She whirled around to see Rebecca.

"My mom was wondering if you'd let us leave some flyers in your shop about food truck night." She handed one for Annie to look over.

"I think this is a great idea. In fact, I plan to stop by

this Saturday after I finish up here. Will you be working?"

Rebecca nodded. "Every Saturday I'm there," she said with less than enthusiasm.

Annie held out her hand for more flyers. "I know what you mean. I do hope you get a chance to have some fun."

"It's hard to find time for that. In fact, I almost forgot what it's like to have a good time." She lowered her gaze.

"Ahh, Rebecca, that saddens me. Well, if it's any consolation, working hard does pay off. One of these days you will have a lot of fun."

"See you tomorrow," Rebecca said as she bolted through the door.

"Good night," she said in a whisper, hoping she was right about the fun thing.

CHAPTER 16

*A*nnie plopped down on the sofa and closed her eyes. She quickly opened them when she heard Buffy whining. "I know, girl. Give me just a few minutes to rest my eyes," she said, barely able to keep her heavy lids from shutting.

You know that deep sleep you get when you first doze off—especially after a very tiring day? Annie drifted there, dreaming of what else, but Jack, when Buffy let out a loud bark, waking Annie out of a deep sleep. Annie opened her eyes wide, her heart beating a mile a minute. She leaned forward and glared at the little fluffy dog. "What was that for? You scared the crap out of me."

Buffy began to dance around the coffee table and

then ran over to where her purple leather leash hung on a hook near the door.

"Really?" Annie pulled herself off the couch and slowly made her way to the leash.

Buffy led the way down the hall and stairs and out the door. Annie giggled when Buffy squatted at the first sign of grass. "Sorry, little girl. You had to go. Next week after everyone is trained, we'll be back on our schedule. Right now, it's just a bit hectic." Annie patted her on the head.

"Ahh, but, Mommy, I want to go with you tomorrow," a man with a deep voice said.

Annie whirled around. "Jack! What are you doing here?"

Jack leaned over and patted Buffy. "I called you, but it went to voice mail, twice. I was concerned."

Annie dipped her head and pulled her phone out from her pocket. "Three missed calls. You, twice and Mary once. I forgot to turn it back on after training."

"How'd it go?" Jack inquired as they walked hand in hand.

"It went really well. I think all of them are going to be excellent bakers. By the way, have you ever been downtown on a Saturday evening and enjoyed the food truck festival?"

"It's been a long time. It's really good. They usually have live music, too." Jack said, squeezing her hand.

"Rebecca's folks own the Cajun on Wheels."

Jack pulled Annie down as he took a seat on a wooden and metal bench. "It's a beautiful evening, isn't it?"

She leaned into him, resting her head on his shoulder. "Yes, it is, but I recall another night that started out much like this one." She turned to meet his gaze. "It ended up with me looking like a drowned rat." She giggled.

"Hey, I was right there with you—drowned rats," he said smirkingly.

"How's Mary doing at the new job?"

"I don't really know. I haven't touched base with Diane yet. We typically meet once a week to go over business details, sort of a working lunch. I will let you know after my next meeting with her." He dropped a kiss on her forehead.

"I'm a little nervous about this guy she met in Italy. He's coming over to see her."

"All the way from Italy?"

"Yep."

"It must be pretty serious for him to do that, don't you think?"

"That's what I'm afraid of. She doesn't need serious, and she certainly doesn't need complicated."

"Well, she's over twenty-one, Annie." Jack lowered his chin and with half-closed lids, waited for her comeback.

"Twenty-one or not, she's living with our grandmother and auntie, and she just started working. I can just hear Grandmother Lilly now." Annie blew out a burst of air and shrugged her shoulders.

"I get it. I have a cousin like that. Between my uncle and auntie spoiling him rotten, and our grandparents at every chance they get, that kid is the laziest I've ever encountered. It's pathetic. And to think, he's twenty-six years old."

Annie watched as a group of laughing young teens walked by. She followed them with her eyes until they were almost out of sight. She glanced at her phone. "I better get back to the apartment. I still have a hundred things to do before bedtime."

"Let me walk you girls home." Jack took Buffy's leash from Annie.

"Where'd you park?"

"Around the corner from your place. I have the limo tonight. I'm scheduled to pick up some tourists that are staying at the Pelican Inn and take them to the airport."

"We have some beautiful places around here. Let's

play tourist one day," Annie said as she laced her arm with his and held tightly.

After a few minutes, they were standing in front of the cigar shop. "Here we are." He handed the leash over to her.

"It was nice running into you this evening. It rounded my evening out just perfectly." She stood on her tiptoes and planted a kiss on his lips.

As she landed back on the bottom of her feet, he lifted her up, leaning down at the same time and finding her mouth. The firmness of his kiss excited her. She parted her lips just enough to make the kiss more passionate.

Jack stepped back, still holding her hands. "That right there, is going to get us both in trouble." He squeezed her hands before letting go, looking off into the distance.

"Jack, you're not afraid of a little ole' kiss, are you?" she asked in a sexy tone.

"No, not afraid of the kiss. Afraid of what will come after that. I don't want to move too fast."

"I know," she said, dropping her head.

He lifted her chin up with one finger. "I didn't mean to embarrass you or make you feel bad. Don't get me wrong. I loved that kiss. I can only imagine what else besides that kiss you have in store for me, for us." He winked.

Annie smiled. "Thanks for walking us home. We'll get together Saturday and try out the food trucks."

"Good night, Annie. Sleep tight." He moved down the sidewalk toward where he said he'd parked the car. Annie watched for a few seconds, enjoying the view of his backside with his arms swaying, shoulders swaggering, and slightly separated thighs commanding the sidewalk as he moved at a slow pace. Annie drew in her bottom lip. Her body temperature told her it was time for a shower. A cold one.

CHAPTER 17

*a*nnie looked up when she heard the door open. "Hello, can I help you?" she asked the stranger.

"I'm looking for Mary McPherson."

Annie walked around from the counter and stood in front of this person inquiring about her sister. "I'm Annie McPherson. Mary is my sister."

"Yes, I know. She told me I could come here and you'd give me her address."

Annie looked the man up and down. Her eyes focused on the man bun he sported. It wasn't every day a man with his hair piled high on his head came into the bakery. "You must be her friend she met in Italy?"

"Yup. Where can I find her at?"

"Whoa, slow down. First of all, I'm not giving you

her address. If she didn't feel compelled to give it to you, why should I? Secondly, what's your name?"

"Jeremy."

"Do you have a cell phone number, Jeremy?"

He nodded.

Annie walked back around the counter and stepped into the kitchen. Morgan was wrapping up for the day. "Strange man out there, beware," she said, whispering as she grabbed a pencil and pad of paper and rushed back out front. "Here, write down your information. I'll see to it that Mary gets it," Annie said.

After Jeremy jotted down his stuff, he handed it back to Annie. "Tell her I'm staying at the Motel 6, north of the city."

"Oh," she said, realizing that was not the best part of town.

"I can't wait to see her."

"I bet."

Jeremy opened the door and exited the shop but not before bumping the large backpack he wore against the doorframe. Annie frowned. *What in the world has Mary done?*

She waited until the coast was clear and then called Mary.

"I can't talk right now. I'm working."

"Okay, but you and I have to talk tonight. Come over when you're done. I'll have the wine chilled."

"Oh, not again, not another big sister talk that involves wine."

"Let's just say, your man dropped by the shop today."

"Jeremy?"

"Who else?"

"What's the problem?"

"He's not right for you, Mary."

"How can you tell that by just meeting him?"

Annie drew in a deep breath and blew it out loudly. "Because he sports a man bun!"

"So? They wear that over in Italy."

"Just stop by tonight." Annie tossed the phone inside her purse. "That sister of mine is going to give me grey hair," Annie said, looking at Morgan.

Morgan shrugged. "He was kind of cute."

Annie raised her brows. "Did you see the man bun?"

"Yeah, it suited him. He probably doesn't wear it all the time."

Annie pursed her lips. "If you say so."

"*I*'m not going to get into it with you about what is my type of man, Annie."

"How long have you known him?"

"I met him when I first landed in Italy. We became friends right away. He makes me laugh."

"He almost made me fall out laughing when I saw the man bun."

"That's not fair, and that's not very accepting either." Mary crossed her arms over her chest.

"Oh, please. I didn't say anything to him about it. Is he a drifter?"

"Well, not really. Actually, he's taking time off from working and traveling around. He'd spent three months exploring Europe when we met."

"How can he afford to do that?" Annie said.

"He has money. Lots of money." Mary uncrossed her arms.

"How'd he come to receive this money?" Annie raised her brow.

"He inherited it."

"Humph. I just don't know. He wasn't very warm to me."

"Well, Mary, if I know you, you probably came off a bit snobby. He was scared."

"Scared? Snobby?"

Mary nodded. "Just give him a chance. He's a really nice guy."

"If he's such a nice guy, why didn't you give him Grandmother's address?"

Mary poured another glass of wine. "Oh, because I had hoped to have moved out by the time he arrived. That didn't work out as I'd planned. More wine?" Mary asked, holding the bottle up.

Annie tapped the rim of her glass. "Yes, please. What's Jeremy's last name?"

"Stark. Jeremy Stark"

"Stark? Is he from around here?"

"Yes, his uncle is Tad Stark."

"Tad Stark the shark. The high priced attorney whose picture is plastered all over town is Jeremy's uncle?"

Mary nodded.

"Why would the nephew of Tad Stark be staying at the Motel 6 north of here?"

"That's easy. He doesn't like to show off his money. He likes to be among the common people. See how they live, be one of them."

"What? That's ludicrous! I've never heard such a silly thing in my life. You may not have to stay at The Ritz, but you certainly do not have to stay at the Motel 6, either. Something is fishy about this, Mary."

"Please don't interfere with my life, Annie. I really like Jeremy and don't want you to scare him off."

"You don't have to worry about me scaring him off. Once Grandmother Lilly and Auntie Patty get a sight of that man bun, we'll all be saying, Jeremy who!"

Mary frowned.

Annie dug into her purse and retrieved the paper with Jeremy's information. She slid it across the table toward Mary. "Jack and I are going to the food truck festival Saturday night. Why don't you and Jeremy join us?"

"That would be cool. You promise to be nice to him?"

"Of course, Mary. I just am trying to protect you."

Mary cocked her head. "Protect me like Grandmother and Auntie Patty do to you? I thought you hated their meddling."

"Touché, Mary, touché."

CHAPTER 18

*J*ack drove them to the festival. Annie tried not to be nosey on top of being snobby, something that Mary accused her of. They were snuggled in the back seat and occasionally a giggle could be heard.

"I hope we can find parking close by," Annie said.

Jack turned the corner and drove two blocks and pulled into a reserved parking spot. Annie shot him a look with widened eyes.

"It pays to know people," Jack said, putting the car in park.

Annie smiled. "I guess so."

Jack and Annie took the lead and walked about ten feet in front of Mary and Jeremy. Annie laced her arm in Jack's, and stretching her neck a bit, began whispering. "What do you think of Jeremy?"

"Too soon," Jack said.

"Do you think he's hiding something?"

"Too soon."

Annie knitted her brows together. "Is that all you're going to say every time I ask you something regarding him?"

"Too soon," Jack said, laughing.

Annie playfully needled him with her elbow. "I've got your too soon right here."

"Let's just enjoy the evening, eat a little food, listen to a little music, and get to know him."

"Well, at least he took his hair down for tonight."

Jack pulled her close. "Stop being judgmental."

"Oh, great. I can add judgmental to the list of snobby and intimidating." Annie frowned.

"Okay, guys," Jack said, turning around and waiting for Mary and Jeremy to catch up. "Whatchya in the mood for?"

"I think we'll just walk up and down and check it out," Mary said.

Annie stepped around Jack and searched the area for a vacant table. "Meet over there," she said, pointing to an empty one. "I'll go save it now." Annie headed toward the table.

Jack and Annie sat down and waited. After a few minutes, Mary and Jeremy joined them, loaded with paper bowls filled with food.

"Your turn," Mary said, smiling.

"I'm going to the Cajun on Wheels truck," Annie boasted.

Jack and Annie met back at the table, Jack arriving before her. She casually scanned the contents of his cardboard containers as she took a seat on the bench next to him. "That looks good," she said, pointing with her chin.

"Some kind of Thai dish."

"It smells lovely. Empanadas and Cajun shrimp," Annie said, pointing to her own food treasures.

Jack turned around when he heard the sounds of an electric guitar tuning up.

"Mary tells me your uncle is Tad Stark," Annie said, not realizing Jeremy had just taken a bite of his taco.

Jeremy, nodding his head, chewed quickly and answered. "Yes, he's my dad's brother."

"So, you're from Charleston?" Annie asked.

"Yes and no."

Annie tilted her head. "Yes and no?"

"My father grew up here and then left Charleston after college. He met my mother in Italy."

Annie exchanged looks with Mary. "I see. Is that

why you are fascinated with Italy, because you were born there?" Mary kicked Annie under the table. "Ow!"

"Sorry, Sis."

Annie rubbed her shin. "Do your parents live here now?"

"Yes, well not far from here. They live on Kiawah Island."

Annie shot a look over at Jack. "Jack's family owns a piece of that island." She sat up straight, squaring her shoulders.

The band started up, and everyone stopped talking.

"Come on, Jeremy." Mary nudged Jeremy, motioning toward the band. She leaned over and picked up her food. Jeremy followed suit, leaving Jack and Annie alone.

Annie chewed her food slowly, thinking about what Jeremy had said. He definitely was leaving out something, if not completely hiding something. "Why would he stay at the Motel 6 when his folks live here?"

"I don't know. Maybe he got in late and didn't want to wake them?" Jack said.

Annie furrowed her brows.

"Maybe they are away on vacation, and he didn't want to stay at the house alone."

"Now you're really reaching. How about because

he's hiding something?" Annie took another bite of her shrimp.

"Just keep asking him questions. You'll uncover the truth soon enough, Investigator Annie." Jack gently plowed into her, shoving her a few inches.

"Oh, here we go. Another title to add to the list."

"Nosey and investigator are the same, but I think investigator sounds better." He smiled, showing his white teeth.

"You have some basil stuck in your teeth," she said, motioning to his mouth.

Jack quickly closed his mouth "Really? Do I?"

"No, just kidding." Annie slapped him on the leg.

Jack pulled her close. "Oh, paybacks are coming. Just you wait." He dropped a kiss on her forehead.

Annie pulled her head back and focused on his face. She studied it in great detail in a few seconds flat. He was perfect in every way. The look of desire evident on his face brought chills to her spine. And when he lowered his mouth to hers, she tasted the sweetness of coconut and spices such as cloves and cinnamon, heightening her desire all that much more. The music playing in the background added to the mood, and Annie, lost deeply in the kiss, didn't want it to end. But end it did.

Jack looked at her with a clenched jaw. He ran his

hand across his chin. "Your kisses do something to me," he said, his warm teddy bear brown eyes melting her heart.

"Jack, just being with you does something to me."

"Hey, guys, we're making another round. Do you want anything?" Mary said, interrupting the sizzling intense moment between Jack and Annie.

"We'll be right behind you," Jack said, pulling Annie closer.

"Jack." Annie put her hand on his chest.

"I thought you liked my kisses," he said with a low raspy tone.

"That's the problem, I do." Annie pushed back from Jack and put one leg, then the other over the bench and stood. "I think we need something sweet." She pulled Jack to his feet.

"Sweet? I was enjoying my dessert right here." He smiled.

"Jack Powell." Annie swatted his arm.

"I'm just keeping it real." He gave in and resisted no more, following close behind.

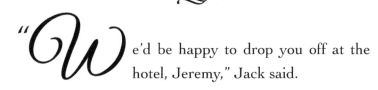

"We'd be happy to drop you off at the hotel, Jeremy," Jack said.

"Or we could drive you out to Kiawah. It's a lovely evening for a drive." Annie squeezed Jack's hand.

Jeremy tossed his head back and laughed.

"If you could just drop us off at Barney's, we'd appreciate that," Mary said.

"Oh, sure," Annie said. "Going out on the town some more, huh?"

Jack pulled Annie toward him, gripping her hand a little more tightly. Annie furrowed her brows.

"No problem, Barney's it is."

Jack and Annie listened to the radio as they drove the few miles back to her place. "I think you're just a bit unkind toward Jeremy. It's a sure way to put a wedge between you and Mary."

The pitiful look in his eyes caused her to turn away and look out the window.

"Seriously, give him a chance." He patted her on the leg.

She whirled around and stared at his hand. He removed it quickly.

He put both hands on the steering wheel, focusing on the road ahead. "Now you're upset with me."

"I'm not upset with you. I guess it'll be all right. I mean she lived over there for the past several months. She was in charge of her own life then. What's the difference?" She batted her lashes a few times and smiled.

"That's my girl. Ease up on her. I bet before the week is over, you'll know everything about Jeremy that there is to know."

Annie quickly gasped and turned her body to face him. He gave her a quick look when he heard her gasp then turned his attention to the road once more.

"I know. Ask Diane to find out."

Jack gave her another quick look. "I can't ask her to spy on Mary."

"Why not?"

"Because, I wouldn't want her to spy on me, or us."

Annie reeled around to face the window again. "You're no fun."

"Oh, I'm not? Did you forget that magical kiss back there already?"

Annie glanced at him over her shoulder. He had the same look in his eyes as he had back at the festival.

"No, I didn't forget." She licked her dry lips.

He pulled up to the front of the cigar shop and put the car in park. She unbuckled her seat belt and scooted closer to him. "Do you really think I could forget a kiss as memorable as that?" She pulled up slightly and kissed his mouth.

"I hope not, because it's all I've been thinking about for the past hour."

"That's all you've been thinking about?" she said, teasing him with her mouth, moving from his lips to his cheek, down his neck, and back to his mouth.

"Annie." He placed his hands on her arms and pushed her back.

She slumped back in the seat. "Yes?"

"You know I can't resist you. If we keep this going, I don't know what I'll do." He turned his body, pushing up against the driver's window.

"Maybe I don't want you to resist me. Have you thought about that?"

"Be careful what you wish for," he said, pulling her back into his embrace and devouring her mouth with his.

CHAPTER 19

*A*nnie beamed with pride on how well her new staff not only picked up the training, but how well they all got along. Now that the cupcakery had a full staff, it finally allowed Annie more time off. Not surprised that Betsy became the mother figure to the younger staff, she shared all the baking tips she had up her sleeve, and she didn't hesitate for a moment to give out orders, in a sweet way, of course.

Annie couldn't help it. She had to stop by, even on her day off. It didn't feel natural to be away from the shop when it had consumed all her time before. "Good morning, Betsy."

"Good morning, Annie," Betsy said as she wiped the flour from her hands on her apron.

"Everything going okay?"

"Yes, Annie, everything is going well."

Annie peeked inside one of the large mixers. She inhaled the batter, closing her eyes as she did. "Strawberry shortcake?"

Betsy nodded. "Yes, it's the new favorite for summer."

"No more salted chocolate caramel?"

"That is still popular, and one that is gaining on it is this strawberry shortcake. Who knows what will be the next fan favorite." Betsy chuckled as she tossed her head back.

Annie glanced at her watch. "I guess I'll leave you to it. You're more than capable. I just wanted to make sure things were going smoothly for you." She backed up a few steps and turned toward the doorway that would lead out to the counter.

"Annie, Morgan is still a big help here, and Rebecca can ring up cupcakes like no one else. And, Peter ... he's super good at his job. Look around. Doesn't the place shine like a new nickel?"

Annie nodded. "Yes, everything looks wonderful. So I shall leave you to it and go visit my grandmother and auntie. They'll be surprised to see me at this time of day. I think I'll take them out for lunch."

"*W*ell, isn't this a surprise," Grandmother Lilly said when she opened the door and saw Annie standing there.

"That's just what I told Betsy you'd say." Annie stepped inside.

"What brings you here?"

"I thought I'd take you and Auntie Patty out for lunch. Maybe you have some errands to run as well?"

Grandmother Lilly quickly placed her hand over her heart. "Oh, that would be lovely, dear."

Annie sat in the formal living room, turning the pages of a magazine while she waited for them to get ready. Her phone vibrated, letting her know she had a call. She looked at the screen and smiled. "Hello, Jack."

"Hey, there. I'm on my way to the airport to pick up a family flying in from Wyoming. Do you think they'll have culture shock?" He laughed.

"Perhaps so, but hopefully in a good way."

"What are you doing today on your day off?"

"Taking Grandmother and Auntie Patty out for lunch and helping them run errands."

"That's nice. Listen, my parents want to have you and your sister over for dinner Saturday night. It will just be the six of us."

Annie quickly made a head count. "Six?"

"You, me, my parents, and Mary and Jeremy."

"Oh."

"You didn't think I wouldn't invite Mary's friend, did you? That would be rude."

"I guess I'm going to somehow have to break it to the two old women today."

"Why? Let Mary do that, in her own time."

"Why must you always be the voice of reason, Jack?" she said, sighing into the phone.

"Remember, step back, let Mary be an adult. If it means she makes some mistakes along the way, so be it."

"You're right. I have to let go. It's just …"

"I know, you've been her big sister looking out for her. It's time she looked out for herself. You did your duty, and your folks would be proud."

Annie looked up when she heard footsteps. "I have to go now. I'll talk to you soon."

"Have a great day. Oh, and Annie?"

"Yes?"

"I can't stop thinking about our kiss the other night."

A grin swept across her face. "Me either."

"We're ready," Auntie Patty said.

"I see that." Annie stood up and admired how nice they both looked.

"Where shall we go for lunch, dear?" Grandmother Lilly asked as she laced her arm with Annie's.

"I don't really know. Any idea, Auntie Patty?" Annie held out her other arm for Auntie Patty to take.

"I've been reading a lot of good things about the café over off of Calhoun," Patty said.

"Okay, let's give that a whirl. Any errands to run?"

"I need to go to the post office," Grandmother Lilly said.

"I'd like to stop at the beverage shop," Auntie Patty added.

Annie pulled her head to the right and tilted it, making eye contact with Auntie Patty. "Out of scotch?"

Auntie Patty cleared her throat. "Now, dear, don't be too nosey. It doesn't suit you." Auntie Patty pointed her chin up and squared her shoulders.

Annie giggled. "You two are a hoot. And I love you both dearly. Now let's go eat."

Spending her day with her family and having a wonderful lunch out, Annie couldn't have asked for a better way to spend her first full day off. She sat on her couch and opened up her laptop. She searched the web a little and then picked up the phone and called Mary.

"Just quickly, because I know you're working. What's your schedule like on Wednesday? I thought I would treat us to a day of pampering."

"I'm off on Wednesday, but Jeremy and I were going to hang out."

"Oh," Annie said with disappointment clearly hanging in her voice.

"But maybe another time?" Mary said, trying to be supportive.

"Okay. By the way, Jack wants all of us to go over for dinner at his parents' house on Saturday night. Can you and Jeremy make it?"

"I'll ask him, but I'm sure it would be fine."

Annie hung up the phone and leaned back into the cushions. She moved her head to the side and stared at Buffy curled up in her bed. She closed the laptop and placed it on the coffee table. *Having days off might prove to be more difficult than I'd imagined.*

CHAPTER 20

The three stood on the Powells' stoop. Annie glanced over her shoulder before knocking. She took a quick look at her own attire and then rapped lightly on the door. The butterflies in her stomach fluttered nonstop. The door opened wide, and there Jack stood, all smiles.

"Hey, guys. Glad you could make it. Come on in." He stepped aside so they could all file in.

"Something smells delicious," Mary said.

"Mom's gumbo and cornbread. I hope you brought an appetite."

After the introductions, the group made their way to the living room. Drinks were served, and chatter ensued. It appeared by all counts that Jeremy and

Mary were hits with the Powells. It brought relief to Annie, and it showed when she relaxed her shoulders.

"Hey, beautiful," Jack said as he gave her a quick kiss on the cheek.

Annie's eyes twinkled, and her cheeks blushed as she soaked up the compliment. "You look pretty handsome yourself."

He raised his drink to hers, and they toasted. "To a great evening," Jack said.

She drew in a taste of the lemony cocktail. "This is really good. You're becoming quite the bartender." She leaned over to give him a kiss when out of the corner of her eye she saw Jack's mother, Milly approaching them. She pulled back just in the nick of time.

"Annie, dear. It's so nice to see you again. How are your grandmother and auntie?"

"They're doing well, thank you. In fact, I took them out to lunch earlier in the week. Feisty as always." Annie smiled at Jack.

"Your sister is so cute. How old is she?"

"Twenty-two. Still wet behind the ears."

"How long has she been with Jeremy?"

"Mother!" Jack said.

"I was just curious if it was serious or not." She raised her brows.

"It's too soon to know that. She met him while traveling in Italy."

"It must be serious then if he came back here to Charleston with her." She drew in a taste of her drink.

Annie shook her head. "He didn't come here with her, he's just visiting."

"I better go check on our dinner."

"I apologize right now for her behavior," Jack said.

"No worries. I'm glad to see that every family has a nosey parker." She laughed.

"But see how irritating it can be?"

"I do. I'm trying hard. Haven't you noticed?"

"I have." He pulled her close. "I think you were about to kiss me before we were interrupted."

Annie leaned over and gave him a kiss.

He brushed his mouth along the bottom of her lip. "Lemon."

"Dinner is ready," Milly said from the doorway.

Annie put her arm around Mary's shoulders. "Having fun?"

Mary nodded.

Over large bowls of steaming gumbo, the table became a lively setting of joke telling, news, and business. Jack's dad lost everyone when he began to talk about the stock market.

Milly saw it play it out before her very eyes and

jumped up announcing it was dessert time. "Annie … Mary …"

The girls followed Milly to the kitchen.

"When he starts talking about the stock market I have to find somewhere to go," Milly said as she sliced the pie. Motioning to the fridge, she said, "There's whipped topping, too."

Mary opened the fridge and retrieved the bowl with homemade whipped cream. She stuck her finger in the bowl and licked it. "Creamy deliciousness."

Milly led the way back into the dining room, pushing the swing doors open with her back. Annie and Mary followed closely behind.

"Dessert!" Milly announced as she set a plate in front of her husband, Robert before taking her own seat.

"Mom, this is so good." Jack slowly pulled the fork out of his mouth.

"Glad you like it, Son."

"Yes, Mrs. Powell, the pie is delicious, and I really appreciate the homemade whipped cream," Annie said as she took another bite.

The rest of the evening went fairly well. A few more questions from Milly that made everyone a bit uneasy, but as Mary reminded Annie once they were out in the car, they had to learn to live with Annie's nosiness, so Milly just prepared them.

"Thanks a lot, Mary. What about Grandmother and Auntie Patty? They're super nosey. I got it from them," Annie said, defending herself.

Mary laughed. "No worries, big Sister. I think Jack's mother is like a lot of mothers."

"True. And grandmothers."

"And aunties," Mary added.

"And big sisters," Jeremy said, chiming in.

"Hey, who asked you," Mary said jokingly.

"Mary, I'm still waiting on our girl day. My feet are begging for a pedicure."

"I know. I'm sorry it didn't work out the other day. Let's shoot for Friday."

Annie pulled up to her parking spot and cut off the motor. "Thanks for coming tonight."

"Sure. Thanks for inviting us," Mary said

"You kids be safe driving." Annie watched as they got into Mary's car.

❧

*A*nnie put the key in the lock and gave it a twist, pushing open the front door. She quickly kicked it shut with her foot. She latched both locks and headed upstairs.

Buffy greeted Annie by jumping up on her legs.

"Hey, girl. Were you a good girl?" She patted her on the head. "Give me five minutes, and I'll walk you."

Annie was grateful she didn't have to walk her too far. She lived in a safe neighborhood, but she didn't like to go deep into the city alone and at night. As Buffy did her thing, she wondered if it might be time to think about a house and yard.

"How'd you like to have your own fenced in backyard, Buffy?"

Buffy wagged her tail.

Annie laughed. She knew full well Buffy couldn't understand a word she'd said. It was all about the tone. She'd read one time you could tell a dog something nasty, but if it was in the baby voice they loved, they'd wag their tail anyway.

After their brief walk, they headed home. They settled together on the couch. Annie didn't make it a practice to invite Buffy up on the furniture, but she felt like cuddling with her. Annie channel surfed before settling on the *Cake Boss* show. Totally engrossed in the concoction that a contestant designed, Annie became startled when her phone went off.

"Just wanted to say good night."

"Aww, that's sweet."

"Can I ask you a question. It just sort of popped into my head tonight while I was walking Buffy. I've been thinking about maybe getting a house and a yard. Anyhow, I realized I don't know where you live."

"I live at home over the garage."

"At your parents place? Doesn't your mother drive you mad?"

Jack laughed. "I have my own entrance, but yes, sometimes she does. Then I get on my boat and stay out all day. I had a plan. It sort of got derailed when I broke up with my fiancée."

"What sort of plan?"

"I had been saving for several years to build our dream house. Then after she called it off, I still had to pay off the rings, pay the vendors and all of the other deposits that came due because of the wedding cancellation."

"Oh, I see. That makes sense."

"I hope by this time next year I'll be moved out."

"Oh, where are you going?"

"To live on the island. I've been saving up to build my dream home."

"How exciting," Annie said

"I could use a woman's touch when it comes to design elements," Jack said.

"I'm sure your mother would be delighted to help you."

"I was hoping you'd help me. I don't want to ask my mother."

"You want me to help you decorate your home?"

"If you would."

"Jack, I'd be happy to. I love to decorate. I was just telling Buffy tonight that it may be time for us to give up the apartment and find a house with a yard. We've outgrown this space," she said.

"And what did Buffy say?" Jack laughed into the phone.

"Stop messing me with, Jack Powell. I know where you live and I can tell your mother," Annie said, snorting in the phone and waking up Buffy.

CHAPTER 21

It had been ages since Annie got together with her girlfriends. Scheduling lunch dates proved more difficult with each passing month. Jessica just had a baby, Cassie was pregnant and finishing her second trimester, and then there was Vicky, knee-deep in her wedding preparations. When Vicky accepted Annie's lunch invitation, Annie couldn't believe her ears.

"Oh, Vicky," Annie said, spreading her arms wide.

"Girl, it's been way too long. It's so good to see you."

"I can't wait to hear about your wedding plans. Are you stressed yet?"

The two gabbed as the hostess led the way toward their table.

"I'm so stressed. But you know, my new favorite saying is, it is what it is."

Annie laughed. "I bet. Well, I can't wait to come and see you two lovebirds finally tie the knot. Soon you'll be Vicky Collins."

"Victoria Collins," Vicky said with a tone of superiority.

"I like the ring of that," Annie said, nodding.

Vicky fussed to Annie about how picking out the right bridesmaid dresses for Jessica, who'd just given birth and still had a few extra pounds to camouflage, as well as one to accommodate the expanding girth of Cassie's tummy, challenged her beyond her wildest dreams.

"I've selected five different dresses at three different stages of planning my wedding. I'm about to just have you as my only bridesmaid. You're not pregnant are you?" Vicky teased as she poked at her salad.

"No, I'm not pregnant. I'm hardly seeing anyone."

Vicky peered up at Annie. "Hardly?"

Annie smiled. "Jack is his name. We really just started seeing each other. He's a great guy."

"Good. Great guys are good." Vicky put her iced tea to her lips and drew in a taste.

Annie nodded. "You know Jessica and Cassie didn't do these things on purpose. They love you, and it's just one of those things."

Vicky forked a beet chunk and put it in her mouth. She chewed it slowly.

"Having a baby is a nice thing. You are happy for them, right?"

Vicky twisted her mouth then relaxed her lips. "Of course, I'm happy for them. It just makes it difficult picking out dresses. Do you realize we went from a fitted knee-length shift to an A-line skirt? Not to mention the color changes."

"I think A-line is still a good choice," Annie said, savoring a spoonful of her chicken gumbo soup.

"Yes, but now the measurements have changed. These changes are costing me money."

"The wedding is in two weeks. You're probably safe with one more fitting."

"Tell me more about Jack."

Annie's eyes lit up. "He's part owner of Powell Limousine Services. Oh, and they also have a vacation rental business."

"I've used his services before."

Annie knitted her brows together. "You

have? When?"

"A while back. In fact, he's providing pick up service for me at the airport for my out of town guests. And I've rented a couple of houses for them to stay at. Diane ..."

Annie widened her eyes. "Diane is his sister. In fact, my sister, Mary is working with Diane now."

"What a small world." Vicky glanced at her watch.

"Do you have to run off?" Annie said, relaxing her shoulders and slumping.

"I do, dear. I have to meet Cassie and Jessica at the dress shop. Thank God you are still the same, and no adjustments are necessary for your dress." She pushed back her chair.

"Lunch is on me," Annie said.

Vicky dug in her purse and fetched her keys. "Thank you. Next time it's on me."

Annie slid her chair out and met her halfway. She reached her arms out and pulled her in for a hug. "Everything is going to be just fine. The dresses will be beautiful, you'll be beautiful, and it will go down as one of the best weddings in Charleston history," Annie said, giving her a quick peck on the cheek.

Vicky drew in a deep breath and let it out slowly. "Thanks for saying that. I really am happy the girls are in the wedding. I just want everything to be perfect."

"It will be. And, you know why?"

Vicky cocked her head to the right.

"Because we've been best friends for many years. We've had our ups and downs, but we all agreed we'd be in each other's weddings. This is just us keeping our promise."

"True, Annie, so very true. Talk to you later." Vicky rushed out the door of the small café.

Annie looked back at her soup and glass of iced tea. She sat back down to finish her lunch. She'd no sooner sat down when her phone started ringing.

"Hello," she said, recognizing the number.

"Dear, you must come quickly and take me to the hospital. There's been an accident and Lilly is hurt."

"What happened?" She gathered her stuff and rushed to the register. She motioned for the clerk to hurry up and ring her up. "I have an emergency," Annie said, covering the phone with her hand.

"I told her not to do it," Auntie Patty said.

The clerk handed Annie her change.

"Do what?" Annie rushed out of the café and found her car.

"To get up on the ladder."

Annie slumped back in the driver's seat. "Ladder? Never mind. Don't tell me. I'm on my way." She quickly started the car and drove off as fast as she could.

hey entered the emergency room. Annie walked up to the counter. "We're here to see Lilly McPherson."

The attendant looked at a chart. "She's in room 6A. If you go over to the doors, I'll buzz you in," she said, motioning toward the secured doors that separated the rooms from the waiting room.

Annie and Patty made their way down the hallway. Full of equipment and staff, the hospital emergency room clearly was busy. Annie stopped in front of 6A. She pulled the curtain open. Annie gulped. She'd never witnessed her grandmother appear so vulnerable. Her eyelids fluttered when Patty pulled a chair out and sat down.

Annie's eyes focused on Lilly's wrapped ankle. "At least she didn't break any bones."

"Thank God," Auntie Patty whispered.

Lilly stirred and then slowly opened her eyes. She blinked a few times and tried to sit up. She grimaced.

"Grandmother, I don't think you should be moving just yet."

"It's just a little sprain. I'll be as good as new."

Annie frowned. "I can't believe you got up on a ladder. What were you thinking?"

"I wanted to get down the box with the photos in it."

"I would have gotten that down for you. Mary would have gotten that down for you." Annie touched Lilly on the arm. "You could have been seriously hurt." Annie's phone started to vibrate. "That's Mary, now." She left the room.

"How's Grandmother?"

"She's going to be okay. Sprained ankle and who knows what else. I've not spoken to the doctor yet."

"I'm coming right now."

"Well, hold off. I don't know if they are keeping her or letting her come home. Stand by. I'll call you as soon as I know something."

"Okay, keep me posted," Mary said.

"I will," Annie said, finishing the conversation with Mary.

Annie entered 6A. "Grandmother, has the doctor spoken to you regarding your injuries?"

Lilly shook her head.

Annie turned her head and lowered her gaze to meet Patty's. "Please stay with her. I'm going to see if I can find the doctor."

Annie stepped outside of the curtain and looked around. She finally caught the attention of a nurse standing nearby. "Hello, I'm Annie McPherson. My grandmother is in 6A."

"She's a sweet lady. Doctor Carlisle saw her," the nurse said as she read the chart.

"Doctor Carlisle." Annie pursed her lips. "What is Doctor Carlisle's first name?"

"Michael."

Just then Annie heard a familiar voice. "Well, if it isn't little Annie McPherson."

Annie twirled around to find standing in front of her Michael Carlisle. "Michael!"

"I thought that was your grandmother in there," he said, motioning toward the curtain.

Annie drew in a deep breath and when she let it out, she sighed loudly. "My very stubborn grandmother, I might add."

"She has a sprained ankle. It could have been so much worse. She also has a bruised elbow."

"And a bruised ego, no doubt." Annie winked.

Michael laughed. "Yup and a little of that. I would like to keep her overnight just to make sure everything is good. Is that all right?"

"Why yes, of course. I appreciate that."

"We're just trying to find her a room. Shouldn't be much longer." He reached out and touched Annie on the arm, sending shivers up her spine.

"Thank you," she muttered.

"You look great, by the way. I haven't seen you for ages."

Annie nodded. "I opened up a cupcake bakery downtown, Sweet Indulgence."

Michael pulled his head back. "You don't say. I'll have to stop in sometime."

"That would be great. Thanks again for taking such great care of Grandmother. If it's okay, we'll stay with her until her room is ready."

"Of course, not a problem." He glanced at his watch. "I'm on break in about fifteen minutes. Care to join me for a cup of coffee in the glamorous hospital cafeteria?" His eyes twinkled, causing Annie to smile.

"Sure, that would be great. We can get caught up."

Michael walked away, and Annie entered her grandmother's curtained off room.

"That's little Michael Carlisle?" Patty whispered.

Annie furrowed her brows. "Were you eavesdropping, Auntie Patty?"

Patty picked up her hand and placed it on her heart. "Who me?" She batted her lashes, and then a wide smile crossed her face.

"Well, I guess you also heard that they are keeping Grandmother overnight for observation. They're getting a room for her now."

"Oh, she's going to hate staying the night."

"Oh, well. She should have thought of that when she climbed the stupid ladder." Annie shrugged.

CHAPTER 23

*A*nnie headed to the cafeteria. She found him right away. It was hard to miss the tall, good-looking man waving from across the way.

He pulled out a chair for her. "Thanks for accepting my invitation for coffee." He pushed her toward the table. "I'll get our coffees."

"What have you been up to, besides baking?" Michael opened a pink package of sugar substitute and stirred it into his coffee.

Annie stirred her cream around and then drew in a small sip of the hot brew. "Taking care of two old women and my sister. You remember Mary?"

Michael nodded.

Annie had a flashback to a time when Michael was

more than just a friend. They'd dated a little in high school and in college.

"How's …" Annie stumbled as she tried to recall her name.

"Jennifer," he said.

"Jennifer. I'm sorry," Annie said.

"We're divorced."

"Oh, I'm sorry to hear that. Any children?" If Mary had been there, she'd have cautioned her about being so nosey.

"No, we were only married for three years."

Annie laughed. "I may not have been very good in math, but that's plenty enough time to have a baby."

Michael drew in a taste of his coffee, nodding as he did.

"Do you remember Vicky, Cassie, and Jessica?"

"Of course. You guys never went anywhere without each other."

"Well, times have changed. Cassie and Jessica are married. Jessica just had a baby boy, Reece, and Cassie is six months pregnant with a little girl. They've picked out a name for her. Katy."

"And Vicky?"

"Vicky is getting married. We're all in her wedding, which is in two weeks. She's been a bit stressed about

the dress fittings. Or should I say all the changes."
Annie took another sip of her coffee.

"Who is Vicky marrying?"

"His name is Scott Collins. He is active duty Air
Force, stationed at the air base."

"So, you're the last of the bunch to get married. Are
you seeing anyone?"

"I just started dating Jack Powell. You probably
don't know him."

"Jack Powell, owner of Powell Limousine
Services?" Michael asked.

Annie's jaw dropped. "Yes. That is so strange to me.
I'd never heard of his services before, yet Vicky and you
have. I guess I don't get out much."

"I know of him because he dated Jennifer."

"He wasn't the reason your marriage broke up, was
he?" Annie's pulse quickened as she spoke the words.

Michael shook his head. "No, he was her rebound."

Annie shrugged her shoulders in a sigh of relief.

Michael reached out and patted her arm. "Your
Jack Powell is a good guy. He put up with a lot of stuff
from Jennifer. I think she broke his heart."

Annie lowered her gaze to her cup and nodded.
"Yes, I think she did."

Michael glanced at his watch. "Well, my break is up.

Let's go see what room they've assigned to your grandmother." He pushed his chair back and stood.

Annie also slid her chair back and stood. Now they were an arm's length apart. "Michael, I'm sorry about you and Jennifer."

"It's okay. It's hard to have a personal life when you're an emergency room doc. I'm used to it."

"I hope you find happiness. You will forever hold a special spot in my heart," Annie said.

CHAPTER 24

*A*nnie smiled over at Jack. He looked extremely handsome in his formal attire. Happy he'd accepted the invitation to accompany her to Vicky's wedding, a warm feeling brushed over her as she stood next to Cassie and Jessica. Soon the wedding march played, and as Annie watched her friend walk down the aisle and exchange vows, she wondered when or if she'd ever stand in that same place.

Vicky had gone all out for her reception. The venue, which overlooked the bay, couldn't have been more perfect. Round tables covered with white linen table-cloths dotted the room.

"I have to sit up there with them during dinner," Annie said, motioning toward the long table up front.

"No worries, I'll be fine," Jack said, pulling her close.

Annie leaned back and smiled. He dropped a sweet kiss on her cheek and then moved to her mouth. She held him in place as he kissed her.

After dinner, the party ended up on the dance floor. When Jack and Annie slow danced, it was the first time they were that close for that long. It felt good to be up against his hard body. She fantasized about what it would be like to be embraced in his arms in a more intimate situation. She blushed at the thought and soon warm waves of desire took over. She held him tightly, nuzzling his neck and taking in his woodsy spice scent. He slowly moved his hands up and down her back, finally resting them on her hips. They swayed to the music, and for the first time ever, Annie felt a connection she'd never felt before. And, she didn't want it to end.

Somewhat shaken by the experience of being so close and connected, Jack and Annie held hands as they made their way to his table. He pulled her chair close to him, and while their fingers were laced tightly, he brought her hand up to his mouth and kissed them, one by one. Another blast of warmth traveled her body and made her more aware of her womanhood, causing her to blush.

"Annie, my beautiful Annie," Jack said, kissing her hand again.

She pulled in a deep breath letting it out slowly. A small breathless whisper escaped her mouth.

"I've been thinking about how handsome you look in that grey suit and baby blue shirt."

Jack's eyes moved up and down as he looked her over. "Your dress is so hot. I love the way it hugs all your curves." He brushed his hand across his chin.

"Vicky was having a major meltdown about these dresses. But I agree, we all wear them pretty well." Annie looked over her shoulder to her girlfriends, who wore the same color but different styles.

"I don't know if I want to take that dress off, or just keep looking at you while you're wearing it. Both are a major turn-on." He laced his fingers with her hands again.

"Jack, you're making me blush."

"Just keeping it real," he said as he made a circling gesture with his thumb on hers.

"I have to admit, I felt something tonight I've never felt before. When you held me in your arms while we danced, it was as if we were the only two on the dance floor. I felt safe in your arms," she said, her breath catching as her heart raced.

Jack looked over Annie's shoulders and smiled. "Bridesmaids, twelve o'clock."

"Oh, Annie," Cassie leaned over and hugged her shoulders. "What a beautiful wedding. And you look so elegant in that dress."

"You look lovely, too. I'm so happy Vicky was able to settle on dresses that suited all of us. The color is what really brings it and ties us all together." Annie ran her hand over the light grey material. "I just love the color."

"I know, right? Jack, you look rather debonair tonight."

"Thanks, Cassie. You look stunning as well."

Cassie ran her hand across her baby bump. "Well, this little package is coming with me for the next three months, so I guess we better get used to it." A warm smile crossed her face.

Jessica walked up to the group, holding a glass of champagne and giggling.

"Someone is having fun tonight," Annie teased.

"It's my first night out since I gave birth." Jessica slurped her drink.

"Be careful. It's probably your first night out drinking since you gave birth." Annie raised her brows.

"This is the last one." Jessica held up her glass before taking another sip.

"Ladies," Vicky said, coming up behind the group.

"Oh, Vicky, your wedding was beautiful. We're so happy we could be part of your special day," Jessica said, sounding a little emotional and maybe a little tipsy.

"Yup, from the ceremony to the reception, it was great," Cassie said.

"I guess we'll be planning baby showers next," Vicky said.

Vicky quickly came over to Annie once she realized what she'd said. She took her by the hand and forced her to come with her. She pulled her through the group and took her aside. "Listen, I didn't mean to exclude you. You know you're going to get married. Maybe to Jack even. When the time is right, you'll know. And honey, your wedding will be the most beautiful of all." She pulled her close for a hug.

A tear rolled down Annie's face. She quickly wiped it away. The champagne had her feeling a bit emotional. "I really like Jack. I think maybe he could be the one."

Vicky held her shoulders and focused on Annie's eyes. "Go with your gut. Don't let him get away if he's the one."

Annie nodded.

"Okay, girls, I'm off to be with my hubby. Thanks again for your contribution. We'll get together after the honeymoon." Vicky gave kisses to all the girls and nodded to the husbands and guests. She went to Jack and leaned over, whispering in his ear as Annie watched on. Vicky kissed him on the cheek and then brushed by them all in her wedding dress, picking up the hem as she made her way across the room to her new husband.

"Well, I guess we'll call it a night," Cassie said.

"I'm right behind you," Jessica said.

"Drive safely," Annie called out.

"Your friends love you," Jack said.

"I love them, too."

"Aren't you curious what Vicky said to me?" Jack asked.

"Sort of."

"She told me if I knew what was good for me, I wouldn't let you get away."

Annie raised her brows and bit down on her bottom lip.

"And do you know what I said to her?" Jack said.

Annie shook her head, still holding her bottom lip between her teeth.

"I told her I had no intention of ever letting that happen."

CHAPTER 25

*A*nnie pulled down the apron from the hook and tossed it over her head, securing it tightly around her waist. She needed something to distract her, and baking cupcakes hopefully would be the diversion she so needed.

"I'm keeping notes. So a few months ago it was chocolate salted caramel, and then we had strawberry shortcake. What's the new flavor of the season now?" Annie stepped up on the stool and grabbed a new bag of cake flour.

"Pumpkin cheesecake," Betsy replied. "Everything pumpkin is all the rage."

Annie nodded. "Pumpkin this, pumpkin that."

The two women worked in unison, each one moving around the kitchen and mixing up cupcake batter. *Who said two women can't work in a kitchen together?* Annie thought back to when she hired Betsy. "How's Rebecca working out?"

"She's doing great. She asks about you all the time. Her infectious smile draws the customers right in, and soon they're coming back for more."

"It seems weird not to come in here more often. You and Morgan have done a wonderful job in making sure the cupcakes are baked and ready for purchase."

The aroma of cupcakes baking made Annie's tummy growl, not to mention making the shop smell amazing.

"These pumpkin spice cupcakes smell so good," Annie said, leaning over and drawing in a whiff.

The bell jingled from the door, and Betsy looked over her shoulder. "It's Jack," she whispered.

Annie wiped her hands on her apron and rushed to the glass display case. "Hey," she said, a warm smile spreading across her face.

"Hello. Wow, something smells delicious."

"Pumpkin spice, our new flavor. Everything okay?"

"Yup. I only have a minute, but I wanted to see your smiling Irish eyes before I headed to the airport."

Annie walked around the long display case and into his arms. She pulled back slightly, looking up at him. "You're so sweet, Jack Powell. How'd I ever get so lucky?"

He planted a kiss on her lips, taking her by surprise. He held her back briefly. "I think I'm the lucky one."

She raised up on her tiptoes and kissed him. She dropped back down, now flat on the ground. She grabbed his hand with hers. "Come on, I'll get you a cupcake for the road."

"Hello, Betsy," Jack said.

"Hello to you, Jack."

Betsy quickly iced a pumpkin spice cupcake and handed it to him. He blinked twice and glanced over to Annie then back to Betsy. "How'd you know?"

Betsy chuckled. "Just a hunch." She winked at Annie.

Annie mouthed "Thank you" to Betsy and then laced her arm with Jack's. "I'll walk you out."

"How's your Grandmother doing?"

"She's doing fine. You'd be hard pressed to tell she'd ever been in the hospital, or had a minor injury. She's back to barking out orders at poor Auntie Patty."

Jack threw his head back and roared with laughter. "Your grandmother, she's a character."

"By the way, she wants us to come over for dinner."

"Jeremy and Mary, too?"

"She asked them, but Mary was quick on the ball. She said she and Jeremy had other plans."

"Well, you need to learn how to think fast like

Mary." Jack leaned over and lightly brushed the top of her head with his lips.

"Seems so." She placed her hand on his arm and left it there.

"My parents have been bugging me about another dinner, too." He placed his hand on top of hers.

"I like having dinner with them. Just tell me when. I know Grandmother and Auntie Patty would like to see them again also."

"Oh?"

"I hear about that every so often as well," she said, smirking.

"Well, she always makes a big deal for my birthday and since it's on Halloween …"

"Halloween is your birthday?" Annie asked in surprise.

"She would like to have a party," Jack said, finishing his sentence.

"I had no idea you were an October birthday. Let's see, that's Scorpio? How old are you going to be?" Annie said, fishing for details.

"The big three oh. And you?"

"Twenty-seven on May twelfth."

"Are we compatible?"

"What do you mean?" Annie said, furrowing her brows.

"You know how they say certain signs are more compatible than others?"

"I don't care what any silly horoscope says. We're more than compatible." Annie reached up and pulled him down for a kiss.

"Hey, watch the merchandise," he said, holding out the cupcake.

Annie reached over and dabbed a bit of the cheesecake icing on her finger and then licked it.

Jack pulled her in for a deep kiss. "More of that later." He glanced at his watch. "I'm late." He ran out the door.

A wide smile crossed her face.

"He's a charmer, isn't he," Betsy said.

Annie whirled around. "Yup, he is. I can't get enough of him. And when he stops by and surprises me, it's the most wonderful moment." She crossed her arms and hugged herself.

"Do you love him?" Betsy asked.

Annie knitted her brows together. "Love. Now that's a deep subject, and I think we have cupcakes to ice." Annie walked back toward the kitchen, a broad smile spread across her face.

CHAPTER 26

Fall moved in as summer crept out, bringing with it cooler temperatures and lower humidity. A welcome change as far as Annie was concerned. All the storefront windows, including the cupcakery's, were decorated with fall foliage and everything pumpkin.

"I love the window, Rebecca," Annie said when she came into the shop to surprise her.

"Annie!"

Annie embraced Rebecca. "The stenciling is so nice. You're very artistic."

"Thank you," she said bashfully.

"Have you tried one of the pumpkin spice cupcakes?" Annie asked.

"Yes, twice," Rebecca said, giggling.

"Buffy and I are taking a nice long walk and enjoying this beautiful day."

Rebecca smiled down at the dog. "Enjoy your day off."

Annie put out her hand to open the door but stopped. She turned toward Rebecca. "Rebecca, how are things here?"

"Good, Annie, very good. Why do you ask?"

"I just want to make sure you're happy."

"I'm pretty busy with school and the food truck. I'll be happy for the day when I can just concentrate on life and not studying."

"Oh, Rebecca, dear. Be careful what you wish for. It's great to be young. Enjoy it while you can. Soon enough you'll be saddled with bills, careers, boyfriends, and all the adult stuff I have to deal with."

Buffy let out a bark. Annie lowered her gaze. "Okay, don't be so impatient. Bye, Rebecca," she said as she pushed open the door.

Annie crossed the street and walked a couple of blocks to the Waterfront Park. She gazed over toward the pier where many people had gathered—older people, younger people, and of course, lovers holding hands. She continued walking, settling on a bench near the famous Pineapple Fountain. The splashing of water as it hit the basin of the fountain added lyrical notes to the stillness of the late afternoon. A few children's laughter could be heard in the distance. Buffy found a spot and laid down, content watching the passersby as Annie did. Annie pulled her sweater closed and buttoned it. After a few minutes of people watching, Annie stood. "Time to head home, Buffy."

Annie smiled at everyone she passed and stopped for the few who asked if they could pet Buffy. What would normally take about twenty minutes took almost thirty, but Annie wasn't in any hurry. She loved her new freedom.

"A cup of hot tea for me and some puppy chow for you," Annie said as she got out Buffy's food.

While Buffy ate, Annie heated her water in the microwave. She opened the pantry and peered at the shelf. She reached for the Moroccan spice tea and at the last minute some crackers. It would be a light dinner tonight. She opened the fridge and grabbed some cheese and olives.

Annie made up a plate with her items, and along with her mug of hot tea, made her way into the living room. She'd just settled down on the couch to watch a little television she'd pre-recorded earlier when her phone rang.

"Hello," she said.

"What are you doing?" Mary said.

"Eating and watching *Dancing with the Stars*. What's up?"

"Grandmother is driving me crazy."

Annie laughed. "Barking out more orders, is she?"

"I'm telling you. First, she wants her foot elevated, then she doesn't. Then she asks me to get her a cup of tea, only to tell me it's too hot and to fetch her some ice. It goes on like that from the time I get home until the time I go to bed."

"Think about poor Auntie Patty. She has Grandmother duty when you're at work."

"I know. I'll just be glad when she can get up and get her own things."

"It has to be rough on her as well. Just think about it. She went from being independent to dependent, overnight."

"Well, if she hadn't gotten up on that ladder—"

"I know," Annie said, interrupting her.

"I'm just frustrated. Then there is Jeremy."

"What's going on with him?"

"We just had our first fight."

"Over what?"

"He wants me to move with him."

Annie leaned forward on the couch. "Move with him to where? I thought he liked it here."

"He did, but now he says it's boring here. He's ready to go back to Italy."

"What did you tell him?" Annie said.

"I told him I couldn't. I told him Grandmother and Auntie Patty needed me."

"Well, they could—"

"And you. I told him you needed me, too."

"Whoa, wait a minute." Annie furrowed her brows as she made sense of what Mary said.

"I don't want to leave Charleston. I missed it while I was gone. Oh sure, living in Italy was great and all, but I like it here."

"Why didn't you just tell him the truth instead of making all of us the scapegoat?"

"I guess because we don't really have a strong relationship. I guess because maybe I want him to go."

Annie gasped. "I thought you cared about him, that the sun rose and set on him. Now, you're telling me you want him to go?"

"Let's just say I've grown up a lot since then."

"Please. Since about three months ago?" Annie laughed into the phone.

"Annie McPherson, don't play with me. I need your help."

"My help?"

"I need you to help me convince him to leave."

"It doesn't sound like he needs much convincing if he's asked you to go with him. Just tell him bye bye," Annie said.

"I told him I'd think about it."

"Okay, let me get this straight. You told him all the reasons you couldn't go with him, but then you told him you'd think about it?"

"He's hard to resist."

"Mary McPherson. See? I can use your whole name, too. What did he do? Kiss you and make you forget what you really wanted?"

"Something like that."

"Okay, first of all, you can't be persuaded by a kiss, no matter how good it is." Annie frowned at her own contradictory words.

"I told him I'd give him my answer by Saturday night."

Annie's eyes darted around the room. "So, we have exactly three days to figure something out."

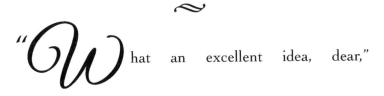nnie moved across the small room and answered the door. "Hi. I'll just grab my things. Come on in." She opened the door wider for him.

Buffy ran up, wagging her tail. "Hey, girl how ya doing?" Jack patted her on the head.

"She thinks she is going for a walk." Annie laughed.

"Maybe tonight after I bring Mommy home." Jack blushed at the tone of his baby talk.

Annie smiled. "Okay, let's go get dinner."

"Who hat an excellent idea, dear,"

Grandmother said, staring at all the little cartons of food.

"Chinese food just sounded good." Annie picked up her chopsticks.

"So, Jack, how've you been?" Auntie Patty asked.

"Good. Busy. It doesn't matter what time of year it is, tourists come to Charleston."

He had that right. In the springtime, they came for the festivals. In the summertime, for the beach, and in the fall, they came for the cooler temperatures, ghost walks, and more festivals. Holidays were always busy as they frequented the open markets and shops in the historic downtown area, or shopped at one of the many malls.

"How are your folks?" Patty inquired.

"Doing well, thanks for asking." Jack winked at Annie from across the table.

"Jack was just telling me it's his birthday on the thirty-first."

"Oh, how nice, a Halloween birthday," Patty said, trying her best to use the chopsticks.

"In fact, my folks want to throw me a party. I'm afraid it's grown from a family dinner to an all-out costume party. I'd like it if you both would attend." Jack's eyes journeyed from Lilly then to Patty.

"It's been ages since I dressed up for a costume party," Lilly said, pouring a cup of the Chinese tea Annie had fixed earlier.

"It sounds like a lot of fun. Count us in," Patty said. She opened her mouth to receive a piece of sweet and sour chicken and dropped it onto her plate. She tossed the chopsticks to the side and picked up her fork. "I'll starve if I have to use these things." She stabbed the piece of chicken with her fork and ate it.

"Patty never did learn how to use them," Grandmother said, picking up rice with hers.

"Show off," Patty pouted.

"Now, you two, settle down," Annie said teasingly.

"Are Mary and Jeremy coming to the party?" Patty wondered.

Annie cleared her throat. "Well, there's a little problem where Jeremy is concerned."

"What kind of problem?" Grandmother Lilly said, raising her brows.

"He wants Mary to move with him, and she doesn't want to go."

"When did that happen?" Jack asked.

"I just found out the other day. She has to give him her answer by Saturday."

"She's not contemplating going, is she?" Patty said.

"No, she wants to break up with him. She's seen the error of her ways."

"I rather liked him and his man bun," Patty said.

"Of course, you did," Lilly said, frowning.

"Anyway, I'm supposed to help her devise a plan, but I haven't been able to completely develop one, except for her just to tell him no."

"Excuse me for butting in, but that is exactly what she should tell him. Just be truthful." Jack reached for the carton of fried rice.

"I know. That's what I thought as well, but Mary is worried he might get upset."

"Upset how? Like scream and yell or like raise a hand to her?" Lilly exclaimed in concern.

"I just think she's worried he'll make a scene and she doesn't really want to hurt his feelings."

"She could tell him she met someone else," Patty said.

"I thought about that as well, but when would she have time? She's with him a lot."

"I have an idea. My cousin Danny can be the decoy. He's a total playboy so he'd jump at the chance to make some guy jealous. We'll tell Mary about him and work out the details. I can have him bump into them somewhere and put on the playboy charm he is known for.

Before you know it, Jeremy will run with his tail tucked." Jack said.

Annie pursed her lips and nodded. "It might just work."

CHAPTER 28

*A*nnie laughed so hard when Mary told her about their little ruse. Having been on the jilted side herself before, a small part of her felt badly for Jeremy, but once Mary gave her all the details that slowly subsided.

"He said that to you?" Annie asked incredulously.

"Yup. He called me a money hungry bimbo."

"He has a lot of nerve. Are you sure he's gone, because if he isn't, I'll sic Jack on him."

"I'm sure he's gone. And you know what else I'm sure of?"

"What?"

"He didn't really care about me. I think he knew I wouldn't go with him to Italy, so that's why he gave me the ultimatum."

"Well, I say good riddance," Annie said.

Mary and Annie locked eyes. The silence in the room grew until finally Annie got up from the sofa and strode toward the window. "I need to go shopping for a birthday gift for Jack and to find my costume. Want to go with me?"

"Do you think Danny will be at the party?"

Annie whirled around.

"He's kind of cute," Mary said.

"He's a playboy. And those were Jack's words, not mine."

"I'm looking for a no strings attached kind of guy."

"Mary McPherson," Annie said, moving toward her.

"Hey, I'm young and single. That's what young and single people do. We date, we break up, we date some more ..." she said trailing off.

Annie opened then closed her mouth. After a moment's pause she spoke. "Well, I don't know for sure if he's going to be there, but I can ask Jack."

Mary grabbed her crossover bag from the back of the kitchen chair. "Let's go."

Annie gathered her things from the table and crossed to the front door. She opened it, motioning for Mary to step into the hall. Annie pulled the door shut.

"A sexy nurse or a sexy maid?"

Annie   frowned.   "You're   incorrigible,   Mary
McPherson."

~

*A*nnie dragged Mary into the bookstore. She
had an idea for a birthday present for Jack.
She examined the different rows, finally settling on a
stack of books.

"What are you looking for?" Mary asked, pulling
out random books and putting them back in.

"A book of house plans."

"House plans? You mean as in building plans?"

Annie nodded. "Yes, he wanted to build a house on
the land their family owns, but it never materialized.
Maybe this will give him the push to do it."

"Well, what makes you think he even has the desire
to build if he never did it before?"

"We've discussed it. He just hasn't been able to find
the right design yet." She leafed through a book and
then closed it shut. "This one is perfect."

"Now can we go to the Halloween store?"

"Let's grab a cup of coffee. I'll call Jack."

They walked up to the counter and ordered two
pumpkin lattes. Mary wanted hers made with almond

milk. A small white mustache formed on her top lip when she drew in a taste of the brew.

Annie walked up ahead as she spoke with Jack. Mary tried to stretch her ear to hear, but it was no use.

"Okay, this is what he said. He said he'll invite Danny, but he doesn't want you to hold him responsible for anything he says or does."

Mary raised her brows. "Ooh, that sounds kind of juicy."

"You've been warned. He is known for loving and leaving them. You could just be another notch on his belt."

"Annie! I'm shocked and insulted you'd think I would give in to his sexiness." Mary winked at her sister.

"Well, I'm having a hard time resisting Jack's sexiness. It must run in the family." Annie nudged Mary in the shoulder.

CHAPTER 29

*A*nnie's breath caught when she saw her grandmother and auntie come out with their costumes on. The flapper outfits were divine and suited them appropriately, right down to the long string of pearls and feathers they adorned.

"You wear the naughty school teacher costume very well, dear," Patty said, nodding to Annie and causing her to blush.

"I wonder what that sister of yours is wearing?" Lilly said.

Annie gulped. She wished she didn't know. "It'll be a surprise, I'm sure," she said, telling a little lie.

"Ta-da," Mary said, stepping out from the hallway.

Lilly and Patty gasped. Annie's brow went straight up to her hairline.

Mary twirled around. "Well?"

Lilly and Patty exchanged looks. Annie tilted her head as she looked up and down at Mary's costume.

"I think you better grab a warm coat," Grandmother said as she put her own on.

There was a slight breeze blowing through, giving the night air the perfect Halloween chill. Children were already making their way up and down the sidewalks, going door-to-door, collecting candy. As the ladies made their way out of the house, Annie turned off the porch light, hoping it would dissuade children from coming up to the stoop.

Annie and Mary helped their grandmother and auntie settle in the back seat and then Mary jumped into the passenger seat upfront.

"You do like my costume, don't you?" Mary asked.

Annie kept her eyes on the road. Children were thick on the sidewalks. "I like it."

"You don't love it, though."

"It's not that. It's just a little skimpy."

"Of course it is. It's supposed to be."

"Well, I'm sure you'll be a hit with Danny," Annie said, staring straight ahead.

*J*ack answered the door dressed in regular street clothes.

"Where's your costume?" Annie asked.

"I'm running late. I'll get changed soon."

Milly had decked the house with orange and black crepe paper and other festive decorations. Spooky music played in the background along with a mixture of other tunes. Bowls and trays of snacks garnished all the tables, and on the kitchen large island there was a black cauldron of witches' brew.

"This is spiked, so be careful," Annie said as she ladled some for her grandmother and auntie.

Milly came up behind Annie and hugged her. "You look so cute in your sexy teacher outfit."

"Thank you," she said, sliding her glasses up and smoothing down her red plaid skirt. *She'd leave the real sexiness to Mary.*

"Ladies, you remember my auntie and uncle?" Jack said as he entered the kitchen.

"Yes, why of course," Grandmother said.

"It's so nice to see you again," Patty added.

"Are your grandparents coming tonight?" Annie tasted the witches' brew and wrinkled her nose.

"They just got here. Come on, I'll seat you with

them." Jack held out his arms to both Grandmother and Auntie. They laced their arms with his and off they went, leaving Preston and Susan Powell with Annie.

"I thought Mary had a boyfriend," Susan said.

"They just broke up."

"She gets over breakups fast," Susan said with a scowl on her face.

Annie crossed the kitchen and peered out into the living room. Mary, practically sitting on Danny's lap, laughed loudly and was clearly flirting. Annie looked back over her shoulder toward Jack's uncle and auntie. "She's young. What can I say?"

Annie left the kitchen and entered the living room. Her grandmother and auntie were in deep discussion with Jack's grandparents on both sides. She smiled to see them having so much fun. She casually moved across the room to Mary and Danny, her eyes settling on the bulging biceps and tattoos on his arms.

Mary withdrew her arm from Danny's. "Hey, Annie," she said with a grin that spelled trouble.

"Can I see you for a second?" Annie raised her brows.

Mary jumped up from the seat and took Annie by the arm and moved her out of ears' reach of Danny. "What's up?"

"Can you button your blouse, please?" Annie motioned to her gaping blouse exposing the roundness of her breasts.

Mary furrowed her brows. "It's part of the sexy nurse outfit."

"I'm a sexy teacher, and you don't see me exposing my body."

"The only thing sexy about your outfit is the length of your skirt. You didn't even wear the garter belt that came with it."

Annie pulled Mary further away from Danny. "It's just we're over here at Jack's parents' house. I just want you to be a little tamer, please."

Mary pulled away from Annie's grasp. "I'm just having fun after a major breakup that has left me sad and blue."

"There you are," Jack said, coming up behind her.

Annie spun around. Air whooshed from her lungs and her heart fluttered. Her eyes moved up and down as she took in Jack's costume.

Mary rushed by Annie, almost knocking her down. She ran her hand up and down Jack's arm. "Oh, my God. You look so hot. I mean fireman hot."

Annie stood dumbfounded. Her stance on sexiness just went out the door. How could she pass judgment on

Mary's sexy nurse outfit when Jack came out in jeans, boots, no shirt, suspenders, and a fireman hat?

Mary ran back over to Danny and left Annie and Jack alone. He pulled her close and whispered in her ear, causing her to blush and a warm feeling run all through her veins. "If my teachers had looked like you, I would have never learned anything." He nuzzled her neck.

"Well, I could say the same for you. I'd call 9-1-1 all the time." She smiled up at him.

He pulled her out of the commotion of the living room and down a dark hallway. He guided her back up against the wall. They laced their fingers as he leaned in for a deep kiss that left her breathless. Her heart quickened as he gently ran his tongue along her bottom lip. She could feel his body pressed against hers and for a few moments got lost in his embrace.

They broke apart when they heard feet shuffling toward them. "Sorry, kids. Have to use the bathroom," Uncle Preston said.

Jack pulled Annie away from the wall. "I guess they will miss us if we don't mingle."

Annie stopped in her tracks. Jack turned back around and took a couple of steps toward her. She batted her lashes and gave him a sexy grin that made him squeeze her hand.

"If you keep looking at me that way, we may never leave this hallway." He pressed a quick kiss to her mouth. "Come on," he said, leading the way.

After a dinner of steaming beef stew and cornbread, Milly brought in the birthday cake, glowing with one candle, the number thirty. The cake with white icing had blue waves and a dock with *Lady Powell* anchored to it. "Not really a cake for a Halloween birthday, but it's fitting for Jack," Annie mused.

They sang "Happy Birthday" to him, he blew out the candles, and then the gifts came out. He received a nice fleece-lined zippered sweater, some dress shirts and neckties to go with his suits, and her grandmother and Patty surprised him with tickets for a scenic helicopter ride. Annie suddenly got cold feet when it was time to give her gift. She handed over the book she had gotten wrapped by the bookstore staff, and then returned to her seat.

Jack smiled. He gently peeled back the paper, finally exposing the book. He flipped through the pages and then closed it. He looked across the room and made eye contact with Annie.

"What is it?" his mother asked.

Jack held up the book. "A book with house plans."

Robert crooked his neck toward Annie. "Good. Maybe now he'll build the house."

Jack pushed back his chair and quickly made his way to where Annie sat. He leaned over and kissed her on the top of her head. He rose up and looked around the table. "Thanks, everyone, for the nice gifts and the great party."

Annie tugged at Jack's suspenders. He leaned over placing his ear near her mouth. "Where're Mary and Danny? I didn't see them get up."

Jack quickly stood up, his eyes darting all around the table. He took off out of the dining area. With her hands clasped on top of the table, Annie waited. Soon Jack stood by her side.

"Everything is okay. I thought for sure I'd find them in a compromising position."

Annie swallowed down the lump that formed in her throat. "Where did you find them?"

"They're outside, handing out candy. You should see them. They are making the kids do tricks in order to get candy." Jack laughed.

Annie slumped forward. Jack placed his hands on her shoulders and gently massaged them. Annie heaved her shoulders up and down. She had to learn to relax. "Jack, I hope you liked the book I got you."

"It was the perfect gift. I can't wait for us to look through the plans."

"Us?"

Jack pulled out a chair and sat down next to her. He took her hands into his. "Yes, us." He circled her thumb with his as he focused on her eyes.

Annie pulled in her bottom lip. "Okay," she said barely above a whisper.

CHAPTER 30

*O*ctober had come in and swept Annie off her feet. She barely had a chance to catch her breath and in came November, bringing with it the holidays. She and Jack had been spending a lot of time together, cuddled on her couch sipping hot chocolate and watching Hallmark movies. She could be such a sap when it came to holiday movies.

"Are you sure you haven't had it up to here with Hallmark movies?" She drew her hand to her neck and made a cutting action.

"Anytime I can cuddle on the couch with my baby, I'll do it." He pulled her onto his lap.

She circled his neck with her arms and urged him in meeting his lips with hers. She pulled back and smiled. "Since Thanksgiving is just around the corner, we probably should talk about dinner plans," Annie said, staying put on his lap.

"My family has been bugging me about it, and we're still three weeks away." Jack kissed the top of her nose.

"It makes sense to have it at your folk's house. They have the larger home."

"Someday we'll be hosting all the dinners." Jack ran his hand up and down her back.

"Jack, what are you saying exactly?"

"I'm saying, or should say, I'm asking you to be my wife."

A wide smile formed on Annie's face. "Jack, are you serious?"

"I would never joke about anything as serious as marriage." Jack patted Annie on her bottom. "I have something."

She moved off of his lap and snuggled close to him, her arm laced in his. Jack dug into his pocket and pulled out a black velvet box. "I had it planned differently, but you know what they say about the best-laid plans." He opened the box.

"Oh, Jack. It's beautiful," Annie said, wiping away the tears that rolled down her cheek. "It's perfect, and the way this happened is also perfect." She held out her hand as he placed the solitaire diamond on her finger.

"Annie McPherson, will you be my wife?"

"Yes! Yes," she said, reaching up and cupping his face. "I love you, Jack. I've loved you for a while."

"I have you beat. I tried to shake the feeling because it happened suddenly, but from the first day I saw you, I knew you were special. By the second time, I knew you were going to be mine." He kissed her mouth and then withdrew.

"I hoped we would become more than just friends, but after my last breakup and yours, I wasn't about to risk moving too fast. I just tried to enjoy every moment we spent together."

"But what was the defining moment when you realized this … what we have, was serious and not just some passing fad?" Jack asked as he moved his arm around her and held her tightly.

"It was the way you gingerly helped my grandmother and auntie get in and out of the car. What about you?"

"Oh, that's easy—the day you served me a cup of coffee with my cupcake."

Annie giggled. "I didn't want you to leave."

*A*nnie flashed her ring to anyone who showed even the slightest interest. She found herself staring at it a lot. Preparations were under way for Thanksgiving, and everyone knew Christmas would come flying around the corner soon after.

She began to feel some stress closer to the holiday. Her hairbrush and shower floor showed signs of hair loss, and like a teenager, she broke out with pimples.

The orders for cupcakes came in by the dozen. Along with pumpkin spice, the new flavor, cranberry, and walnut with cream cheese frosting became the next most ordered flavors. They found it difficult to keep up with all the holiday madness. When Annie turned the sign to closed, she drew in a deep breath, filling her lungs to capacity and raising her shoulders as she took in the air. When she emptied her full lungs, her shoulders relaxed.

~

*G*randmother Lilly and Auntie Patty insisted on making a dish for dinner. They were busy in the kitchen when Annie stopped by.

"Something smells wonderful," Annie said, peering inside the oven.

"Baked mac and cheese," Patty said.

"Jack is going to love that," Annie said.

The timer went off, signaling to the ladies the entrée was done. Using oven mitts, Annie lifted the large glass casserole dish out of the oven.

~

Milly went all out for Thanksgiving dinner. The house draped in holiday splendor, including the tree all aglow with twinkling lights, greeted them as they entered the house. The heat coming from the fireplace along with the aromas of a baking turkey with all the trimmings warmed Annie's heart and her spirit.

Jack smiled when he saw the ladies' macaroni and cheese dish. He teasingly took it from Annie. "This is all mine," he said.

"The turkey smells delicious, Milly," Annie said.

"It's the one meal a year that takes me all day to prepare and about fifteen minutes to eat. Then there is the cleanup," she said, shaking her head.

"One of these days, we'll be the hosts and take this work off of you," Annie said, hoping her words of kindness brought a smile to Milly's face.

"I'm all for that, how about you, ladies?" Milly directed her attention toward Lilly and Patty.

"What can we do to help, now?" Lilly said.

"The table has to be set. The china and silver are over there," Milly said, motioning toward the tall oak china cabinet.

Annie and the ladies set the table, and soon everyone crowded around, inhaling all the good smells that wafted from the table and kitchen. After Jack's grandmother Wiggins said a blessing, they dug in to eat. Chatter ensued about everything from the weather to Jack and Annie's upcoming wedding.

"I thought a summer wedding would be nice. I always wanted an outdoor wedding."

"Not too late in the summer or you'll be a hot mess," Patty said, chiming in.

"Auntie Patty, that's not very nice," Mary scolded.

"Well, it's true. The heat and the humidity will zap your energy, not to mention your hairdo."

The group laughed.

"How about spring, early May?" Annie nodded as she looked around the room.

Jack reached over and patted her on the leg. "I think May sounds great."

"Will you be able to get everything planned, ordered, and reserved by May?" Milly wondered.

"Not this May, next May," she said, lowering her voice when she clarified herself.

"Oh, I just presumed ..." Milly said, trailing off.

"Mother, I never said any specific timeframe. We have a lot to discuss. We're going to build on the property overlooking the bay." Jack puffed out his chest as he dug into the mashed potatoes.

"Finally. We'll have a vacation home," Danny said.

Jack put his fork down. "No, not a vacation home — Annie's and my home. You'll be welcome to visit and even stay the night, but it'll be our home." Jack looked around the room as all eyes were on him. "It is still mine to build on, correct?" He looked directly at his mother and grandmother.

"Yes, dear, of course."

In no time the conversation became lively with various topics discussed. When it turned to Mary and Danny, Annie could sense her embarrassment when she witnessed Mary's cheeks turn bright red.

"Oh, to be young again," Annie muttered.

Lilly raised her glass. "Here, here."

After a filling dinner, Annie, Jack, Mary, and Danny told the older folks to go in the living room and rest. "We'll get the dishes done and bring dessert in later," Annie said, shooing them out of the dining room.

Mary and Danny removed the dishes from the table

and scraped, Jack stored all the leftovers in containers, and Annie rinsed and stacked the dishes in the dishwasher.

Jack came up behind her and laid his chin on her shoulder. "You smell good."

Annie whirled around. "Thank you. It's called Beautiful."

"Well, how apropos, Beautiful perfume for a beautiful person." He touched her lips with his.

"Don't let Mother stress you out regarding wedding dates or plans."

"I won't, but I just want to make everyone happy. You see how vocal my grandmother is."

Jack laughed. "We have a very opinionated lot. I like the idea of a May wedding. It will give us plenty of time to get the house built. How do you feel about having the ceremony on our little island?"

Annie's eyes widened. "You read my mind. I even thought if we didn't have it finished we could put up some of those big white tents, rent tables and chairs, and strings lights all around and through the trees. I even know where I would want us to stand for the ceremony."

Jack cocked his head to the right.

"By the big magnolia tree in the middle of the land. It would be a perfect place to stand and say our vows."

Jack wrapped his arms around Annie and held her tight. "They say things happen for a reason. That sometimes we have to go through difficult times to get to the good." He pulled back from her.

"I know it. I feel the same way. I've had some pretty devastating things happen to me, but once you came into my life, they just became a memory. You, Jack Powell, will be the new shining light, the light that will lead us to happiness." She pulled him in for another kiss.

"Hey, you two, break it up or get a room. We have dishes to do," Mary said, snapping the dish towel at Jack's rear.

CHAPTER 31

*A*nnie had not been this excited about Christmas in a very long time. She put the little harness on Buffy and her sweater and hooked up the leash. She'd wait for Jack downstairs. That's how excited she'd become over one of the holidays she'd always dreaded before.

She'd only waited for a minute when Jack pulled up. He jumped out of the van and opened the door for her. "I'd say someone is excited about cutting down a Christmas tree." He gave her a quick peck on the cheek.

While Christmas carols played in the background, Buffy curled up into a ball and rested on the back seat.

"Our first Christmas tree," she said, beaming with happiness.

They walked up and down the beaten down trails

looking at all the trees. Annie stopped in front of one. "This one. I want this one."

"It's kind of big. Do you think it will fit in your apartment?"

Annie turned and looked straight up. "I guess it is kind of big, but look how pretty it is."

"Let's keep looking," Jack said.

Annie looked left and right, up ahead, and around the corner. Finally, a tree caught her eye. "Over here. I found it."

Jack walked toward the tree carrying the ax. He nodded. "Now, that's a perfect tree."

After the tree farm employee helped Jack load the tree and secure it, Annie and Jack went back inside for a cup of warm cider and chocolate chip cookies. The little store had a potbellied stove in the corner providing heat. Annie rubbed her hands together.

"I didn't even think to invite your grandmother. She probably would have liked to pick out a fresh tree."

"She buys one every year from the Boy Scouts. I'll drive her over to their lot where she'll pick out the most homely looking tree there. I'll try to convince her not to, but she'll insist. It's our ritual, every year."

Jack laughed. "You mean a Charlie Brown tree?"

"A step-up from that, but it's still pretty sparse."

"Well, maybe there's a reason she picks scrawny trees?"

"Oh, there is. It's not a very good one, though. She claims if she doesn't get it no one else will, and because they've already been cut down, it will die in a heap in a corner somewhere."

"She has a great imagination."

"She just enjoys being dramatic. But, she really decorates these little trees up to look pretty, so maybe she has a point."

"I say let her do whatever makes her happy." Jack drew in a taste of the warm cider. "We must learn how to make this for our Christmas celebrations." He leaned over and kissed her on the mouth.

She ran her tongue over her bottom lip. "Spicy and hot," she said, raising her brows for dramatic effect.

"Spicy and hot, huh? Is that how you like your men, too?" He nudged her arm.

"You could say that." She tossed her head back and drank the last of her cider, throwing the paper cup in the receptacle nearby. "Let's go." She winked.

He tossed back his drink and swallowed it down fast. She wouldn't have to ask him twice.

"*O*kay, a little to the left … oops, now lower the top, okay, steady, come in," Annie said, directing Jack with the tree. "Okay, just a little bit more … good, you're at the stand."

"I can't see the stand. Help me guide the trunk into the ring."

Annie got down on her knees and helped put the trunk in the ring and then secured it by tightening the screws. They stood back and admired the tree. "It's leaning just a little," Annie said, tilting her head.

"Go back down and loosen the screws," Jack said.

"Ahh, now that's a gorgeous tree," Annie said as she wrapped her arm around his waist. "Glass of wine?"

"Sounds good. Let me find some Christmas music." He scanned the radio stations, finally tuning into one playing "Silent Night."

"Here you go," she said, handing him his glass.

"To our first Christmas together," he said, clanking her glass. Jack wrapped silver garland around his neck and danced around. "I'm ready to decorate the tree whenever you are."

Annie grabbed the box of lights. "I love you, Jack."

"I love you, more."

Decorating the tree took teamwork, and Jack and Annie were a great team. She'd toss the string of lights around the tree, and he'd catch it, and they worked the lights around and around until the last string hung on the branches. Annie watched as Jack carefully placed each ornament; his meticulous attention to detail evident in every placement.

Annie and Jack plopped down on the couch. Annie pulled up her legs and rested her feet on the coffee table as she admired the tree. She turned toward Jack and smiled. "We do good work."

He patted her on the leg. "Yes, we do."

"Jack?"

Jack took his eyes off the glowing tree and studied her face. "Yes?"

"We're going to be okay, right?"

He turned his shoulder into the couch, now facing her. "Why would you ask me that?"

"Things seem so perfect. I'm scared."

Jack reached for her hand and held it tightly. "Don't be scared. I promise to love you until the end of time. We'll have our ups and downs, but I promise you, I'll never hurt you and will do everything in my power to protect you."

A tear formed on her bottom lid.

"Don't cry, hon. I mean it—things are going to be great."

"I wish my folks were here to see how happy I am."

Jack softened his features and pulled her close. "I know, baby. I wish they were here, too. But you know, my folks think of you as their second daughter. Everyone loves you. And, you have your grandmother and auntie, and don't forget Mary." A small smile formed on his mouth.

Annie giggled. "How could I forget any of my great and very eccentric family? And yes, your family has been so nice to me and my motley crew." She squeezed his hand.

"Our wedding is going to be a big party. I can't wait." Jack said.

"Do you think it's too far off? I mean I guess we could move it up?"

"I'm good with moving it up, and I'll wait if that's what we have to do. Of course, the wait will kill me," Jack said, his sultry eyes making Annie shudder inside.

"I probably could get things ready by this May if we want to have it on the land. No reservations required," she said, laughing at her own joke.

"True. And I know someone who could provide the wedding cake." Jack smiled.

Annie gasped. "In fact, I thought we'd have cupcakes for the guests and have Betsy make a small cake for the top."

"I know a lot of people here in town who can hook

us up with canopies and chairs," Jack said, getting more excited by the moment.

"Okay, let's do it! Let's get married this May by that glorious old magnolia tree. We mustn't let time escape us, for no day is promised. I want my grandmother and auntie to be present."

"Annie, that sounds great. Let's start greasing the wheels now, and we'll pick up full steam ahead as soon as the holidays are over." Jack leaned in and kissed her.

Annie turned back and leaned against the sofa. Jack did the same. Still holding hands, listening to Christmas music, Jack and Annie steadied their eyes on the festive tree.

CHAPTER 32

*J*ust as Annie said, Grandmother picked out a scrawny tree. It made her happy, and Annie came to realize happiness meant different things to different people. It brought a smile to her face and in turn, to Annie's. The holidays were filled with gatherings of every type. Annie took her employees out for lunch and gave them each a Christmas bonus. It was the very least she could do.

They all met at one of the restaurants down by the pier. It was a spectacular day for early December with the sky the color of robin's-egg blue. The warm temperatures made it a perfect day on the water. Annie waited in the lobby for everyone to gather.

When they had all arrived, the waiter seated them at tables draped in white linen.

"Please, order anything you want. Let's have a wonderful team celebration," Annie said.

After they enjoyed a great meal, she made a little announcement.

"First of all, I want to thank each of you for your outstanding service to Sweet Indulgence. I couldn't have done it without you. From Peter, for keeping the shop in top shining shape," she said, looking at him. "To Rebecca, for your great customer service," she said winking at her. "To Betsy, our chief baker, and to Morgan, who has been with me from the beginning. Each of you has brought a level of talent and professionalism I'm so grateful for. From the bottom of my heart, thank you." She handed them each a card. "Just a little something to hopefully make your holiday a little brighter."

"It's been a pleasure working for you, Annie," Betsy said.

"You've been the best boss and so understanding, too." Rebecca flashed a warm smile toward Annie.

Morgan stepped forward and cleared her throat. "Annie, thank you for being such a flexible boss. I could never have kept up with my school schedule if you hadn't been."

"Yup, what they've said. Thanks for giving me the job," Peter said.

"I'm so glad you all feel that way. I have a bit of news to share with you. As you know, Jack and I are engaged, and we've set a date — May tenth!"

"Congratulations!" they said in unison.

"I have a favor to ask of you all. Betsy, instead of a traditional wedding cake, Jack and I want cupcakes, but we want a small cake for the top. Could you bake the small cake for us?

A wide smile appeared on her face. "Of course, Annie!"

"Peter, we're going to need tables, chairs, and canopies set up. If you could work with Jack and his team, I'd be forever grateful."

Peter gave Annie a playful salute.

"And, Rebecca, I was wondering if your family would like to cater the reception? I know it's a big task, but I thought maybe some of the other food trucks might want to get in on the action. If you could just ask for me, I'll follow up on any leads."

"I'll ask right away," Rebecca said.

Annie rolled her head toward Morgan. "I know you're finishing up finals, so I totally understand you'll be busy," she said trailing off.

"Oh, I'm sure I can do something. I'll put my head together with Rebecca."

The Christmas lunch proved more successful than

Annie could have imagined. Everyone conveyed their best wishes and agreed with her plans, giving her the confidence once again, life was good and precious, and Jack in her life made it all worth it.

∾

Grandmother and Auntie Patty insisted on having an open house. They'd felt a bit left out during all the holiday parties. Annie and Mary rolled up their sleeves, and everything from polishing the silver to dusting the chandeliers in order to prepare for the day, took place.

"Okay, let's go over the menu," Grandmother said, scratching her head under the scarf covering her hair.

"Miniature quiche, pinwheel sandwiches, and dip are what I have," Annie said, looking over her notes.

"I have egg rolls, cheese tidbits, and salami roll-ups," Mary said.

"I'm making sausage balls in barbecue sauce," Patty said.

"We'll have plenty of booze on hand," Lilly said.

Mary, Annie, and Patty all looked up at once.

"Well, we have to have spirits. It's a holiday party, for gosh sake!"

"I think we'll have plenty of food. Betsy is making chocolate chip and oatmeal cookies."

"Oh, that's so nice of her," Mary said, doodling on her paper.

"Okay, so we all have our assignments. I can do the grocery shopping and will drop off your ingredients. I'll make my stuff at my apartment and bring it over in stages." Annie straightened her back and squared her shoulders. "Any questions?"

Mary put down her pencil. "Oh, you are so like Grandmother." She winked.

"I'll take that as a compliment," Annie said, grinning.

"Oh, one last thing. How many people are going to be floating through and did you give them the time?" Patty asked.

"Good question, Auntie Patty. Yes, so I told Jack's family to spread out their visit. I asked my staff to come during another set of times. The neighbors around here have been asked to drop in first. There might be some overlap, but people should move through quickly. The whole idea of an open house is to say hello, wish us well, grab a cookie, and move on," Annie said.

"And have a drink. We must have a toast to the holiday," Lilly added, lifting her shoulders and smiling.

"Yes, Grandmother. A toast to you and the holiday," Annie agreed.

~

The holiday open house went without any hitches. Everything came together as Annie had planned. From the tasty food, to the company, and even the spirits, the party would go down in memory as a success. As all of Jack's family visited, the same remarks could be heard, "What a lovely home ... How nice of you to organize this ... The food is delicious ..." and on and on. Even though her grandmother and auntie enjoyed being the hostesses to the holiday event, everyone knew it was Annie who had made it all happen.

Jack came up from behind and whispered in her ear. "I know this wouldn't be possible if you didn't organize this." He kissed her earlobe.

"It's bringing such pleasure to them. It was the least I could do. They feel sometimes getting old also means getting tossed aside. I didn't want them to feel like that."

"Agreed. I'm so happy you love them as you do. Makes me hopeful for when I get old and grey."

Annie whirled around. "I will love you no matter what. And just for the record, I think you'll be one handsome old man." She leaned in and kissed him on the mouth.

"Well, if I'm going to be one handsome old man, you're going to be one hot old lady." He patted her on the bottom.

"Jack Powell, this kind of behavior can get us into trouble." She wrapped her arms around his neck.

"Good. That's exactly what I want it to do." He found her mouth and devoured it, kissing her passionately.

CHAPTER 33

*A*fter a long and very exhausting day of visiting everyone, Annie finally had Jack to herself. She turned on the lights to the tree, lit some candles, and made sure soft music played in the background. She'd just taken the quiche out of the oven, but something told her they probably wouldn't be eating. The Powells had offered a spread of food that could have fed an army and then Grandmother and Auntie Patty had gone overboard, too.

"Your family was so generous with gifts," Annie said.

"I told you they loved you."

"I hope they liked mine."

"Are you kidding? That's one of their favorite restaurants." Annie handed Jack a mug of eggnog.

Jack put his nose to the glass mug with the Santa stencil on it. He raised his brows. "Brandy?"

Annie nodded. "Just a splash." She snuggled down into the sofa cushions, pulling her legs underneath her. "New Year's Eve is the next hurdle. I'll be happy when all the celebrations are over with, and I can concentrate on our wedding."

"Me, too. I have to get over to the property and check on a few things."

"Oh, what sort of things?"

"The well, for one. It probably will require some work."

"There is electricity, right?"

"Yes, but that's another concern. We have a lot of trees on the property, and it has become quite over-grown. I need to hire some guys to go over and clean out all the underbrush and make sure the power lines are not tangled up in a bunch of branches. It's been on my to-do list for some time. When we went out there during the summer, I got a chance to look around. It's been lurking in the back of my mind since then. It has to be done, and well before the wedding."

"A bad winter storm is predicted for next week. I hope everything will be okay," Annie said, concerned for the first time something might ruin their perfect plans and future.

"Don't worry. I'll get out there. And another thing … we need to get the road paved. Right now it's just gravel."

"Maybe we're pushing this too fast. Do you really think we can be ready by May tenth?"

"Baby, I'll do everything in my power to make sure we are more than ready." He leaned over and waited for her kiss.

Annie leaned in and kissed his warm mouth. She playfully licked her lips. "Tastes pretty good on you," she said, laughing.

He took her mug and set it down, then placed his mug next to hers. He pulled her onto his lap. She wrapped her arms around him, enjoying the view of his gorgeous smile and eyes. "It's not really safe to be alone with you, considering how I feel about you."

"Why do you say that?" She teased him, knowing full well what he meant.

"Because, when I'm with you, I'm my happiest, and well, my happiness spills over to desire. I know we're not kids and we've both been around the block …"

Annie pulled back her shoulders and frowned.

Jack play smacked her arm. "Okay, some of us have been around the block a few times. But, I can't stop thinking about your gorgeous body and how long and lean your legs are. And how the touch of your skin tantalizes me and stimulates my every desire to be with you. It's like a drug, and I can't get enough." He pulled her head down to his. "I love you, Annie. I love you so much." He kissed her lips, and she melted into his arms, inviting him in, teasing him with her tongue, and yearning for more.

She pulled herself away from Jack and rolled off of the couch. The look in her eyes told him she wanted him and so much more. Annie's prediction the quiche would not be eaten until much later came true.

Ravenous from their time together wrapped in each other's arms, the quiche satisfied their hunger while thoughts of being in each other's arms warmed her soul.

"Thanks for being a trooper about going to Vicky's New Year's Eve party."

"Why do you say that? I like Vicky and her husband, what's his name again?" Jack laughed out loud.

"Major Scott Collins."

"Oh, that's right. He's an officer in the Air Force."

"Yup. I hope she realizes what she's getting into. I see a move in her future."

"Surely, she knows marrying someone in the military, a move is not only possible but probable?"

"I think she's just so much in love with him that she has blinders on, but let's not worry about their marriage. Let's concentrate on our upcoming wedding. So, New Year's Eve party at Vicky and Scott's and then full steam ahead for the McPherson and Powell wedding."

Jack pursed his lips and tilted his head to the right.

"What? Why are you looking at me that way?"

"We haven't talked about it before, but the way you said McPherson and Powell, I wondered if you were planning on not taking my last name."

Annie squared her shoulders and focused on Jack's eyes. "Well, to tell you the truth, I was contemplating doing a hyphen."

"Oh, Annie and Jack McPherson-Powell?" Jack said, mulling it over. "I think it has a nice ring to it. Sort of like Vicky and Major Scott Collins," Jack said as he puffed out his chest and bellowed their names.

"No, silly, just Annie McPherson-Powell, you'll still be Jack Powell."

Annie leaned over, placing her elbows on the kitchen table and cupped her face. Jack leaned in and kissed her full mouth. "I'm still going to call you Annie Powell."

CHAPTER 34

*A*nnie turned one way and then the next as she admired her trim figure in the mirror. If she said so herself, she looked hot in the red dress she'd bought especially for the New Year's Eve party at Vicky and Scott's. She ran the brush through her golden red locks, slipped her feet into the black shoes with three-inch heels, and gave herself one last look in the mirror. "Oh, my jewelry," she said as she made her way to the leather case that sat on her dresser, the one she'd received from her father when she was a teen. *It belonged to your mother,* she recalled him saying. She pulled the bottom drawer out and peered inside—touching the pearl earrings, moving to the gold hoops, and lastly putting her fingers on a pair of silver dangly ones with a touch of bling. "These will be perfect with this dress,"

she said as she put them on. She opened the top of the jewelry box and pulled out the matching necklace. She gazed over at the picture of her parents and thought about how pretty her mother must have looked with the jewelry on.

A light rap at her front door brought her back to reality—the harsh reality that both of her parents were gone.

"You look beautiful in that dress!" Jack said, pulling her in for a kiss.

"You look dashing in your tuxedo," Annie said.

"Well, we are going to Major Scott Collins' house," Jack said.

"Will you stop it? You haven't gotten a chance to know him yet."

"Well, I got the impression he thought his you-know-what didn't stink."

"Jack, that's not nice. He probably has a lot on his mind. He's in the military with a lot of responsibility. Stuff is happening all over the world."

"There's my girl, defending even strangers. Your love of humanity is special." Jack kissed her on the cheek.

"I just think we need to give him a chance. He's married to one of my best friends, and most likely, we'll be socializing with them."

Jack cut her a wide-eyed stare. "Wait a minute. You didn't tell me that. I didn't sign up to be bestie friends with the Major."

Annie pouted. "I just thought it would be nice to hang out with them."

Jack softened his stare and broke out laughing. "I had you."

Annie swatted his arm. "Jack! That's not funny. I thought we were having our first argument."

Jack pulled Annie into his arms. He ran his hand down her back and left it resting just above her butt. She liked the way his hand felt and it reminded her of their closeness earlier in the week. "I love you, Annie, remember that. Never let go of that. No matter what the storm, we'll weather it. I promise."

She batted her lashes a couple of times as the words resonated with her. A tear formed in her eye. Not because of sadness but because of so much love and happiness. "Jack, I never knew love like this was possible. You fill my heart with so much goodness. I love you, too."

A mingling of aromatic scents wafted throughout Jack's car. She made sure she'd spritzed on hers and now his, favorite perfume, Beautiful. She tried to figure out what he wore but finally gave up.

"Okay, I give up. What cologne are you wearing?"

"You like it, huh?" He gave her a quick look before steadying his eyes back on the road.

"I love it. It makes me want to …"

"Pull over to the side of the road?"

Annie sighed loudly. "Yeah, that, too."

Jack laughed. "Man, you just can't keep your hands off me, can you?"

"What about you? You can't resist me either, right?"

"Oh, don't even get me started. I didn't even want to let you out of the apartment. Pulling over to the side of the road is an option, though." He gave her a quick wink.

"Turn right at the next light," she said, giving him directions to Vicky's.

A song came on the radio that intensified the romantic feeling she'd already tried to suppress, making it even more difficult to concentrate on directions or anything else, for that matter. Her stomach tightened and then relaxed. Chills ran up and down her arms. A tingling sensation traveled all through her body as she recalled Jack's loving embrace and tenderness. She studied him as he drove; the lyrics to the song driving her wild inside.

"Okay, copilot, how much longer?"

Annie puffed a short blast of air out. "Oops! We passed the street we were supposed to turn on."

Jack pulled over to the curb and put the car in park. He turned his body slightly in the seat with one hand on the steering wheel. Annie focused hard on his face.

"Annie ..."

Annie unbuckled her seat belt and slid across the seat, wrapping her arms around his neck. She pulled her hand up and ran it through his wavy hair. She found his mouth and devoured it, not letting him say a word or come up for air. She kissed him with all the passion she had stored up and then some. He groaned softly low in his throat, and she felt his desire building. He put his hands squarely on her shoulders and gently pushed her away.

"Wow. Okay, that was way better than I expected." His breathing was heavy and labored.

She brushed her hand across her hair and lifted it off her neck. "You can say that again. I don't know what came over me."

"You only did what I was thinking."

She leaned in and kissed his warm mouth. "I love you, Jack. I can't say it enough, and I can't show it enough."

"Oh, baby, you're doing a great job on both. And as much as I'd like to continue our make out session, I think we have a party to get to."

Annie slid back over to her seat. "Okay, make a U-turn. We're just a few minutes away."

Jack followed her directions, and they arrived at Vicky and Scott's just a few minutes late. When Vicky opened the door, she found them holding hands and sneaking kisses.

"Well, well, well. Glad you guys made it. I was beginning to worry about you."

"We're only a little bit late," Annie said.

"Looks like you guys made a detour." Vicky motioned to Jack's face.

Annie placed her hands on his face and turned him toward her. She laughed and then took her wetted finger and wiped the lipstick off his cheek. She turned back toward Vicky and giggled.

Jack leaned over and whispered in Annie's ear. "What? What did I have on my face?"

"Red lipstick."

"Oh." Jack squeezed her hand and then leaned over and kissed her. He whispered in her ear as he made his way to her mouth, "I hope there weren't any cameras on that street."

It was a lively party full of good cheer and the winding down of the holidays. Jack and Scott, or as he liked to call him, Major Scott Collins, developed a friendship despite Jack's earlier displeasure, growing stronger as time went by. Annie smiled when she saw them huddled in the corner, talking about sports, boating, and more. On the way home, Jack told her all about his new friendship and Annie couldn't have been happier. After all, Major Collins was married to one of her dear friends.

At midnight, the group toasted to many years of happiness and love. When Jack turned to Annie to give her his special toast, he laced his arm with hers, while each held a flute of champagne. He stared into her eyes and like another moment she'd experienced with him before, she felt as if they were the only two in the room.

"Happy New Year, Annie. I can't wait for our special day when we become husband and wife. I promise to love you until the end of time."

"Happy New Year, baby. I love you, too, and I promise to make you the happiest man on earth. Please know I might get a little stressed over the next few months while I plan our wedding."

He leaned in at the same time she did, and they kissed as confetti flew over their heads, horns blew, and in the background, "Auld Lang Syne" played, followed by Three Dog Night's "Joy to the World."

CHAPTER 35

*O*ver the course of the next few months, there were baby showers, baby welcoming parties, and wedding showers. Not to mention bachelorette parties. Wedding parties had been decided long before the date. In fact, while they were in college dreaming of the big day, it'd been decided. The four of them would be in each other's weddings and no matter what part of the country they lived in, no matter what was going on in their lives at that moment, they'd agreed—more like pinky swore, they'd be there.

For someone who wore pretty much the same thing during her days at the bakery, shopping for wedding dresses was about as high on her list as going out on one of her Grandmother's setup dates.

They took turns being the supportive girlfriend. You

know—the one that says every dress looked good and it was *the one*. Mary was the only one with the kahunas to tell her the truth.

Shaking her head, Mary scowled. "Nope. That makes you look bigger than you are."

Annie patted her tummy. "I think I've been indulging in one too many cupcakes."

"Try on this one," Mary said, running her hand down the off-the-shoulder, silhouette A-line dress with just a little bling gathered at the waist. Annie took the dress and entered the dressing room.

Annie's smile lit up the entire dress shop when she stepped up on the raised box and twirled. "I like this one!"

"Yes, that's the one. You look stunning in it."

"Yay, I'm done with wedding dress shopping," Annie said, stepping down and making her way toward the dressing room.

"Wait! Shoes—you might as well try on shoes, too," Mary called out with a glimmer of tease in her eyes.

"*O*kay, I'm going over my list here," Annie said, looking at her phone. "I think we've completed everything or at least it's in the stage of being completed."

"What's left to do with the reception?" Mary asked as she bit into her hamburger.

"Betsy is making the cake and the cupcakes. Rebecca's folks are providing the catering, and well you already know Jack's cousin Danny is providing the music. By the way, how are you two doing?" Annie asked, looking up from her phone.

"Just perfect. He makes me laugh, makes me hot …"

"Mary McPherson!"

Mary giggled. "Hey, I'm just keeping it real."

"Well, you better keep that little part from your grandmother and auntie, or before you know it, you'll be going out on dates they've set up for you!"

Mary threw her head back and laughed. "Oh, please. I put a stop to that right away. I told them if they didn't stop setting me up, I'd bring back Jeremy."

Annie and Mary laughed so loud that people began to stare. Annie lowered her voice. "I'm so happy to have you here, Mary. You make my life much better. I mean it."

"Don't go getting all sentimental on me. But, yup, Sis, I love ya too."

~

*A*nnie called a meeting at Sweet Indulgence with the key players involved with the wedding and reception. A task of this size required supervision.

"Okay, everyone. Pull up a chair. I'll try not to keep you long," Annie said to the crowd who gathered around her.

"Rebecca, do you need anything from Jack or me regarding transporting the food to the island?"

"I think we have it covered. We'll be bringing two food trucks equipped with everything we need to make the food, and what we can't prepare on site, we'll be bringing up already made."

"Okay, now remember, it's a narrow road coming onto the property. We have to make sure we're not causing a traffic jam. We'll be having tables and chairs delivered, too. Let me check ... yes, chairs, tables, and canopies will be delivered on Friday at ten o'clock."

Rebecca looked down at her phone's screen. "Food trucks should arrive no later than ten o'clock on Saturday, so that will be just fine."

"Okay, next on the list. Peter, you're going to meet Jack, Scott, and Danny on the island on Friday afternoon and get things set up, correct?"

Peter nodded. "Yup."

"Betsy, the cake?"

"I'm on it. I will have five dozen cupcakes iced and ready to transport along with your small but pretty wedding cake."

"Okay, so we need a volunteer to help transport the cupcakes," Annie said, looking over the crowd.

Peter held up his hand. "I can do it. I'll bring them up on Saturday morning. I told Jack I'd come back out early on Saturday to make sure everything was finalized. We may need extra time. Especially with all the lights you want to be strung up," Peter said, smiling.

"Okay, Peter, thanks, that will be fine. Maybe you can store the cakes in one of the food trucks?"

"That would be fine," Rebecca confirmed.

Morgan raised her hand. "Yes, Morgan?" Annie said.

"I feel badly I haven't volunteered to do anything."

"Well, don't feel bad. You helped me seal and apply postage to all the invitations and then you walked them to the post office. That was very helpful."

"I know, but I'd like to do something for the actual wedding."

"I'll tell you what. I'm sure we'll need an extra pair of hands to make sure the food line goes smoothly. Can I count on you to help there?" Annie nodded as she smiled.

"Yes, absolutely!" Morgan puffed out her chest, happy she'd found purpose at Annie and Jack's wedding.

"What about flowers, Annie?" Rebecca said.

"Mary's on it."

A gasp from the circle made her look up from her notes. "What?" She looked around the room.

"Mary. Flowers," Betsy said almost to a whisper.

"True, she may not be the best choice, but I'm running out of people to task," Annie said cocking her head and shaking it.

"I can help her," Morgan said.

"Thank you, Morgan. Let me know if the arrangements get to wacky. I wrote out all of the details, but we all know Mary."

A chuckle came from the room followed by low chatter.

"Okay, sounds like we have a plan. Thanks again for coming in on such short notice. Starting Friday, I'm giving all my employees time off to attend the wedding. You don't have to report to work until Monday. Be sure to check the schedule in the back room. See you at the wedding!"

~

*A*nnie glanced at her watch. Jack would be over any minute. She rushed to the bathroom and peered at herself in the mirror. "Ugh! Dark circles." She reached for the concealer and dabbed it under her eyes. She ran the brush through her golden red locks, and just for good measure applied a sheer lip gloss. "This will have to do."

A light rap at the door told her he'd arrived. She opened the door and motioned him to enter. He kissed her mouth as he dashed by. "I got orange chicken and fried rice," he said, setting the containers on the table.

"Sounds good. I'm exhausted."

"It'll all be over soon," he said with a spark of happiness in his eyes. He opened his arms wide.

Annie walked over to him slowly with her head hung low. She walked into his arms and breathed in the smell of his shirt. The aroma, a mixture of laundry soap and his aftershave, comforted her. He held her tightly, letting her savor the moment. Truth be told, she could stay there forever.

She pulled away from his hold and kissed him on

the mouth. "Remember, I warned you I'd be stressed out. This is me—stressed out."

"I know, but it's almost over with. Things are moving along. The deliveries are all set and everything is a go. Just breathe."

Annie slumped into his arms. "I'll be so ready for the honeymoon."

"I have an idea. Remember when I told you we used to camp out on the property when I was a teen?"

Annie nodded.

"Let's camp out there tomorrow night. It'll only be Thursday and we can have one last quiet night together before the madness on Saturday. I'll bring firewood and lanterns, and a two-person tent. It'll be fun."

Annie crossed her arms and rolled her eyes.

"What do you say? I know you're the adventurous type," Jack said.

"Have the porta potties been delivered yet?" Annie asked, uncrossing her arms.

"They're scheduled to be delivered Thursday afternoon."

"Okay, it does sound fun. I'll bring the marshmallows, you bring the wine."

*T*hey cuddled around the roaring flame on the beach, roasting marshmallows. The sounds of the waves lapping toward them soothed them, along with the light breeze rustling through the marsh and trees. The hoot of an owl nearby let them know they weren't the only breathing creatures there tonight.

"This was a great idea. Just what we needed before tomorrow," Annie said, feeding Jack a marshmallow.

"How'd you know I liked burnt marshmallows?" He laughed a deep belly sort of laugh, which in turn made Annie laugh.

"It did get a bit toasty," she said, laying the long-handled fork down.

"Oh, look, a shooting star," he said, pointing up toward the sky.

"Could the night be any more gorgeous?" she said, resting her head on Jack's shoulder.

He breathed in the salty air and let it out slowly. "I agree. It's so darn peaceful out here, I just could live here forever."

Annie lifted her head. "We *are* going to live here forever. I can't wait for our house to be built. It will be the place everyone comes to for dinner. It will be the place everyone comes to when they want to have a bonfire on the beach. It's going to be *the* place for well

… everything." She leaned in and kissed him on the cheek.

He pulled her in when she tried to move away. "I love you, Annie, with all my heart."

She leaned in toward him, her lips brushing his. She began to move away but he held her head in place, moving his hand through her hair as he deepened the kiss, caressing her softly. Their tongues danced as their bodies melted together, and then in one swift movement, he pulled her on top of him with the two of them rolling onto the sand. She pressed her hands against his chest as she gazed into his eyes, her breath catching as she studied his hungry eyes. The fire flickering in the background added a level of ambiance to an already intense night. "Jack."

"Uh huh," he said as he trailed openmouthed kisses along the underside of her neck.

"I love you, too, with all my heart."

He played with the wispy tendrils of her hair that fell into his space. "Shh, no more talking," he said as he pulled her in for more kisses.

CHAPTER 36

Grandmother Lilly and Auntie Patty insisted the rehearsal dinner be at their house. Annie and Jack wanted to go to a nearby restaurant. It would have been less stress and less hassle Annie had told them. At least they'd had the good sense to have it catered. They'd just finished dinner and were going over the details one last time when Annie's phone rang.

Annie rarely shouted and especially into her phone, but when she got a call saying the wood dance floor they'd reserved was lost in transit somewhere, she lost her cool.

"How does one lose a wooden dance floor?" Annie screamed. "I don't want a refund. I want the darn floor. I have music planned with dancing. It's my wedding reception, for Pete's sake!"

Jack held out his hand. "Let me talk to them," he said, mouthing the words.

Annie reluctantly handed him the phone.

"Hello, this is Jack Powell, the groom. Listen, I know my fiancée didn't really mean to scream in your ear, but she's a bit stressed right now. See, first the delivery truck had a flat tire on the one-way bridge to our property, and it took us a few hours to change the tire and get it moved. So, we're already behind on setting up canopies, tables, and chairs. Then, when we opened the forty million boxes of twinkling lights, half of them didn't work. So, when she gets a call saying the dance floor is missing, it just made her a little crazy."

"Uh huh, I see. Yup ... right, okay. Thanks so much." Jack handed Annie her phone back.

Annie pulled her brows together, and with one hand on her hip, stared at Jack. "What was that about?"

"I just handled it. A new dance floor is on the way."

"Where could they possibly find another dance floor this late?"

"That's not our concern. They did, and I'm happy. Be happy, too." Jack smiled.

"I'll be happier when I see it," Annie muttered as she walked away.

"I love you," he called out.

～

*T*alk about wedding jitters. Annie had them bad. If Jack had them, he concealed it well. He was as cool as a cucumber Vicky had noted.

"You look absolutely stunning. Jack is so lucky." Vicky stood admiring Annie in her wedding gown.

"I can't believe this is happening. I'm finally marrying the man of my dreams." Annie's eyes glistened with tears as she spoke.

Cassie and Jessica entered the adjoining tent. "Everyone is seated," Jessica said.

"It is so lovely out there," Cassie said, pointing in the direction of the venue.

"It's just as you planned, Annie," Vicky said.

Annie turned when she heard a small commotion coming from the far end. Grandmother and Auntie were having a lively discussion.

"Grandmother and Auntie Patty, what in the world are you guys arguing about?"

"She's insisting I take your left arm. I want to be on the right side."

"Does it really matter?" Annie said with her hands on her hips, eyeing her grandmother first then her auntie Patty.

"In the rehearsal, I was on the right," Grandmother stated.

"Auntie Patty, please, just be on the left. It really doesn't matter. Both of you are giving me away, and that's the important thing," she said, taking her hands off of her hips and crossing toward them. She reached out and lovingly caressed their arms. "You being here today is so special. The stress is real, so please, let's not add to it. You," Annie said, nodding to Grandmother, "will be on my right, and you," nodding to Auntie, "will be on my left."

Grandmother and Auntie nodded. Annie leaned in and kissed them each on the cheek.

In the distance, the music played, letting them know it was time.

"Okay, girls, this is it. Are we ready?" Annie opened her arms wide.

Vicky, Cassie, and Jessica rushed to her arms. "Let's do this," they yelled.

"Wait, where's Mary?" Annie peered over the tops of their heads. She spotted Mary sitting down, quietly dabbing her eyes with a hanky.

"Mary, honey, what's wrong?" Annie couldn't believe it would be anything too terrible. Not on her wedding day.

Mary moseyed over to the group with her head hung low. "I'm sad."

"Sad about what?" Vicky asked, a bit perturbed over Mary's apparently juvenile behavior.

Annie lifted her chin toward Vicky and gave a slight shake to her head, letting her know to ease up. "Mary, what's wrong?"

"I guess it just hit me. Here we are on one of the happiest days of your life, and Mom and Dad aren't here to see it." She wept loudly, heaving her shoulders.

"Oh, dear, please don't cry. You'll mess up your makeup," Annie said lightheartedly. She'd felt that way, too, but decided to forgo getting in touch with her feelings for fear she'd be a total mess walking down the aisle.

The three ladies moved out of the circle so Annie and Mary could have a private moment.

"I'll let them know to give us a few more minutes," Vicky said, stepping out of the tent.

Annie nodded her way.

"Mom and Dad are watching us. They're here with us today. Don't you think for one second they aren't. Be strong, Mary. Be strong for me, be strong for our guests, and for Jack. He's an emotional wreck today, as well," she said, stretching the truth.

"I'll try."

"You have to pull yourself together. We've been through some crappy stuff in our young lives, but this … this we should be jumping up and down in happiness over. I'm marrying Jack Powell, the most wonderful man on this earth, the love of my life."

"You're right. It just hit me, and I couldn't shake the blueness. I'm better now." Mary stiffened her shoulders and smiled.

"That's my girl." Annie leaned in and kissed Mary on the cheek. "Remember, you're not losing a sister, you're gaining a brother."

"And a big family. The Powells have been so sweet to me," Mary said.

"Yes, indeed. I love the way our families have merged as one."

Annie raised her chin and looked up. The girls all herded back inside. "Okay, we've stalled them all we can. Jack is getting suspicious. Are you ready to rock this wedding or what?" Vicky said.

The girls all raised their hands in the air and on the count of three gave a high five.

After the girls left the tent, it was time for Annie to make her entrance. Annie held out her right arm for Grandmother and Auntie Patty took her left.

"What you said to Mary a few minutes ago touched

our hearts. You're a blessing to this family, Annie McPherson," Grandmother Lilly said.

A small smile appeared across her mouth, and with each of them by her side, Annie made the march to her place in front of the most beautiful magnolia tree she'd ever laid eyes on. Even through her veil, Jack's intense look sent chills down her spine. The setting couldn't be any more perfect, and with her best friends and loving family by her side, Annie married the man of her dreams, Jack Powell.

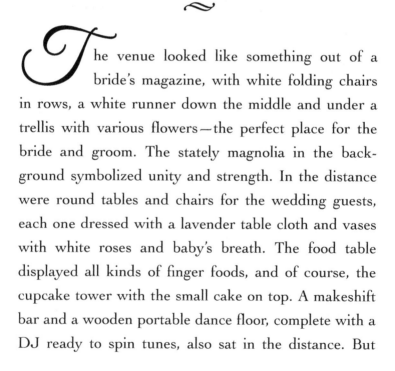

The venue looked like something out of a bride's magazine, with white folding chairs in rows, a white runner down the middle and under a trellis with various flowers—the perfect place for the bride and groom. The stately magnolia in the background symbolized unity and strength. In the distance were round tables and chairs for the wedding guests, each one dressed with a lavender table cloth and vases with white roses and baby's breath. The food table displayed all kinds of finger foods, and of course, the cupcake tower with the small cake on top. A makeshift bar and a wooden portable dance floor, complete with a DJ ready to spin tunes, also sat in the distance. But what really made the event special were the hundreds of twinkling lights strung throughout all the trees.

"Congratulations, Jack and Annie," Vicky said, holding on to Scott's arm.

"It was a beautiful ceremony, and I really like how you did this here on the property," Scott said as he looked around what once was just a piece of land with trees.

Annie thought back about the mayhem earlier in the week over getting the venue prepared. "Well, thankfully, Jack keeps a cool head in emergency situations. I wasn't quite sure how it would all turn out."

"The view is gorgeous. I mean your home will be so fantastic with the view of the bay over there and the trees over there," Vicky said, motioning to the areas as she pointed them out.

"I can't wait to start building. In fact, right after the honeymoon, we're breaking ground," Jack said, putting his arm around her shoulder and pulling her close.

"The front porch is going to be right over by that magnolia tree. I want to come out of my front porch every day and see it as a reminder of our special day," Annie said.

"There's lots of work to be done, that's for sure, but I'm committed, and this will be the house of our dreams when I'm finished."

"Jack and Annie," Milly said, coming up from behind and hugging them.

Robert stuck his hand out to Jack. "Congratulations, Son."

"Thanks, Dad."

"It was a beautiful ceremony. I'm still crying," Milly said.

Just then Danny, in his role as DJ, made an announcement, letting the guests know to get some food and to be ready for toasts.

Annie watched as her in-laws and friends and family made their way to the buffet line. A broad smile escaped her mouth, and she giggled.

"What are you giggling about?" Jack wondered.

"I'm just so happy! I've dreamed of this moment for a long time, and now it has happened, I guess I'm trying to make some sense of it."

Jack pulled Annie into his arms and focused on her eyes. "I wanted to ask you something."

Annie nodded. "Okay."

"You helped me name my boat, *Lady Powell*, and it's a fine name. What about our home? It's going to be unique sitting up here on this beautiful piece of property with the view of the Charleston Harbor in the distance, the waterway below, and these beautiful moss draped trees. Start thinking of a name for our homestead, okay?"

Annie turned toward Jack with her hands clasped in front. "It's funny you mentioned that. I have been thinking about a name already. I can visualize it now. It will be a handcrafted wooden sign made from one of the artisans in town."

Jack nodded, waiting for her to go on.

"Sweet Magnolia."

Jack unclasped her hands, taking them into his own. "Sweet Magnolia ... I like it. So, we have Sweet Indulgence, the bakery, and Sweet Magnolia, our home. I can't wait to see what names you come up with for our children." He squeezed her hands and winked at her.

"Children? Well, how about the family dog first?" She laughed.

Jack's eyes twinkled. "I know just what kind of dog I want to get, too. Do you think Buffy will be intimidated by a large dog?"

"Are you kidding? Buffy can hold her own." Annie laced her arm with Jack's and proceeded to enter the party zone. "Oh, look over there. Rebecca and Michael Carlisle are getting cozy," Annie said.

"Isn't he a little old for her?" Jack said with concern wavering in his tone.

"I think she's older than Mary and Mary is with

Danny. By the way, I've been meaning to ask you. What do all the tats on Danny's arm signify?"

"He got a wild hair when he was stationed overseas."

"Oh, I didn't know he was in the military. Mary hasn't filled me in," Annie laughed.

"Just four years. It was enough to mess him up a bit. I think that's why my uncle and aunt spoil him so much."

"Well, as you know, my dad was in the military. It can be a terrifying thing, especially for a young man."

"He'll work it out. Danny's a smart young man. Maybe Mary will be the one to help him." Jack pulled her in close. Jack motioned toward the back table with his chin. "Speaking of those two, look over there."

Annie's eyes widened when she saw them in a major lip-lock. She shook her head. "Incorrigible."

"Our families—they're just perfect, aren't they?" Jack said, pulling her close.

"Perfect in every way," she said, turning slightly and kissing him.

EPILOGUE

The wedding reception went on until after midnight. Jack and Annie made sure everyone made it to their cars safely. Peter volunteered to shuttle guests in the borrowed golf cart to their cars, which were parked on the other side of the small wooden bridge, in a makeshift parking lot. One by one the two food trucks left. Then the entire wedding party and some remaining friends broke down the tables, chairs, and other props they'd rented and loaded up the delivery truck. Everything came down a lot faster than it went up. The twinkling lights were the only things left and Peter said he'd do them the following day.

"Thanks for sticking around and helping us tear down the party," Jack said.

"I bet Grandmother and Auntie Patty are exhausted," Annie said, covering her mouth as she yawned.

"I think our work is done here. Let's go home. We have an early flight tomorrow," Jack said, helping her up from the chair.

~

*H*e carried her over the threshold even though he'd told himself he'd do it again when they checked into the villa. Annie wrapped her arms around his neck and the corners of her mouth turned up. He took her straight to the bedroom and gently placed her on the bed.

"How about we conserve on water and take a shower together?" He began to loosen his tie and pull his dress shirt out of his pants.

Annie closed her eyes. "Sure, that sounds good," she said barely audible.

Jack went into the bathroom and turned on the shower. He poked his head out of the doorway to let her know the water would be at the right temperature soon and she could begin undressing. "Annie, dear, the water …" He grabbed a towel off the rack and covered himself while walking over to the side of the bed where he'd left her. He gently shook her. Her eyes fluttered but she never opened them.

Jack sighed. "I love you, Annie." He chuckled as he moved to the bathroom where he then stepped inside the glass enclosed shower and turned the temperature to cold.

~

A note from the author:

Don't feel too badly for Jack. In book two of the Charleston Harbor Novels, Sweet Magnolia, Jack and Annie are having a grand time while on their honeymoon in beautiful wine country, California. When they return, Jack begins to build their dream home. Follow along and enjoy the series, as the Powells and McPhersons build a life together.

ABOUT THE AUTHOR

A USA Today bestselling author, Debbie writes sweet contemporary romance and women's fiction. She lives in South Carolina with her husband and two dachshund rescues, Dash and Briar. She loves to hike, work in the garden, and on most sunny days you can find her enjoying her backyard. She's an avid supporter of animal rescue, and as such, pledges to happily donate a percentage of all book sales to local and national rescue organizations. When you purchase any of her books, you're also helping animals.

To find out more about Debbie, check out her website at https://www.authordebbiewhite.com

BOOKS BY DEBBIE WHITE

Romance Across State Lines

Texas Twosome

Kansas Kissed

California Crush

Oregon Obsession

Florida Fling

Montana Miracle

Pennsylvania Passion

Romantic Destinations

Finding Mrs. Right

Holding on to Mrs. Right

Cherishing Mrs. Right

Charleston Harbor Novels

Sweet Indulgence

Sweet Magnolia

Sweet Carolina

Sweet Remembrance

Others

Perfect Pitch

Ties That Bind

Passport To Happiness

The Missing Ingredient

The Salty Dog

The Pet Palace

Billionaire Auction

Billionaire's Dilemma

Coaching the Sub

Christmas Romance – Short Stories

Made in the USA
Middletown, DE
17 December 2020